The Grand Illusion

A NOVEL

STEN HANKEWITZ

To my parents.
For better or for worse, you made me what I am.

FOREWORD

As long as I can remember, I always wanted to become a writer. Actually, that's a lie. When I was five or six years old, I wanted to become a bus driver. There was this bus parking lot nearby where we lived, and I used to go there, asking the bus drivers, "May I steer?", meaning, could I sit on the driver's seat and just do dry steering—a make-belief game for my own amusement to feel like a real bus driver.

In fact, I think the first phrase I learned in the Russian language was, "May I steer?" Most of the bus drivers were Russians and they didn't know a word of Estonian—my native tongue and Estonia's de facto national language. The year must've been 1984 or 1985. Give or take a few.

I distinctly remember that I started writing before the age of ten. In Estonian, of course. I wrote short stories and started probably some 20 novels—at least that's what I thought they'd be. One time, when I told my mother that I wanted to publish a book, she asked, "What, titled 'Elliot's beginnings'?"

And it was true. I may have suffered from attention-deficit hyperactivity disorder—even though, at the time, no one in the East even knew what the fuck that was. But I was a restless kid, I had hard time finishing things I had started because I got a new idea, and thus needed to move on to it immediately, without finishing the one I had already started.

Well, I did finish one. Back then, the best way to get published was to type your writing up, on a typewriter and all, and send it to a magazine. I did just that—it was a weekly youth magazine—and they published it.

They printed it over a few weeks of issues and, boy, was I proud. I didn't realize this actually made me a published author, but the fact that a magazine had seen something I wrote fit for printing, that made a hell of a bragging point.

The trouble was, I had no one to brag to—the few friends I had didn't care much as they were interested in other things, and the people who weren't my friends would give even fewer shits. So, I was pretty much alone with the knowledge that I had written something worthy of publishing.

The thing with growing up is, however, that the older—and supposedly wiser, although that's not always the case—you get, the more idiotic your stories from the past sound. For example, a fifteen-year-old me would be awfully embarrassed over something a ten-year-old me had written. And so was the case with the "novel" the magazine had published—I literally couldn't believe my brain had come up with something this horrid. Not only the plot, not only the style, but also, how bad the writing was. If there had been an award for bad writing—kind of like the Darwin award that's given posthumously to people who had died because of their own idiocy—I would have definitely deserved one of those.

I'm not even sure what pushed me to writing. (Much later, in high school, my literature teacher did, but even more than that, she pushed me to read the books I really didn't want to, so I didn't appreciate her at the time.) Was it that I was an avid reader? Ever since I mastered the skill of reading, I had a book in my hand.

And what else was there to do for a kid in the Soviet-occupied Estonia? Not much, I can tell you that. So ever since I could read, I would sign up at my local children's library and borrow as many books as I could, and I would read them from cover to cover, as quickly as I could.

Of course, since it was the Soviet Union and the Communist Party controlled everything, the choice of books was very limited. There was an ample choice of Estonian writers, translations from Russian and other Soviet languages, but the selection of Western books was scarce. Most Western authors were too bourgeois for the Soviet censors, so they didn't even get translated. My window to the Western writers' creations opened much later.

For many years, however, I stopped reading altogether. As the literature teacher I mentioned earlier pressed me to read tens of books in the official curriculum during my three years of high school, I felt the need to protest and refuse. I wanted to read, but I wanted to read the books I had chosen, not some fucking bureaucrats high up in the ministry of education. That feeling—to be made to do something I absolutely didn't want to—pushed me away from reading altogether for years. Also, there was always something better to do.

But in time, the yearning for the feeling when your eyes rest on well-formed written thoughts came back. And also the realization that the way one can become a good writer is not only sitting down and writing, but also endlessly consuming others' written texts. Not to mention how much you can absorb information from them and educate yourself. And I wanted to at least become a writer, even if not a good one.

Am I a writer now? Fuck if I know. You be the judge of that.

***

Just to be clear, all names in this book are changed and Americanized. You wouldn't have found any Simons, Roscoes, Coreys, Maggies, Janices or whatnot in Estonia, especially during the Soviet occupation. (Things are different now. You'd find a Billy Bob somewhere in the countryside. Smoking oregano—because weed is illegal—and voting for the far-right because, hey, they are the ones who'd legalize weed, right?). I wanted to write this book for the people who speak, read, and understand English.

Also, many people featured in this book would probably not be happy to find out they were complete and utter assholes—even if they're not assholes now, or just different kind of assholes—but still assholes. (Yeah, sure, I'm an asshole myself. But I'm a very different kind of asshole. I think. Maybe even hope.) So, out of respect, and out of my desire to protect myself from whatever these assholes and non-assholes may think after reading this book (well, some of those assholes, I'm sure, can't read, so no harm done there), the people featured here may remember themselves, but other people won't know they're those assholes.

I'm also going to be writing about my parents, grandparents, and great grandparents. My grandparents and great grandparents have all departed this world, so they wouldn't have to read this and feel somehow outed or portrayed unfairly.

My parents, however, are alive. Hopefully, they will be by the time this book gets published and long after that. But I'm going to be honest about them, too. I love my parents, but at an arm's length. They helped form me into what I am today. So I've got to be honest about them.

And my family and my friends—former, present, future—will have to understand that this is how I'm seeing things. They aren't always as rosy as they seem. And they aren't always as gloomy as they seem.

But also bear in mind this isn't an autobiography. This is a semi-autobiographical novel. Some things here really happened—and some didn't. I have a vivid imagination, and this here is a product of that. Take it as a fictional novel about someone who grew up in the Soviet Union—something most of y'all can't even imagine—and the newly-freed small Northern European country you haven't even heard of.

***

My name is Elliot Schmidt. I'm a literary character and I only exist in my own fucked-up head.

THIS IS A TRUE STORY. WHILE IT ISN'T.

BUT IT IS.

MAYBE.

1

The little house on Gutter Street in the Estonian capital of Tallinn—or, well, the capital of the Soviet-occupied Estonia at the time—had stood the test of time. It had been bombed during World War II and half of it had burned down. It was rebuilt after the war and it had ten apartments: some were one bedrooms, some, maybe, two bedrooms. And some were studios as well.

Before the war, it was owned by some rich—or maybe not so rich—real estate mogul. But when Estonia got occupied by the Soviet Union, private ownership of pretty much anything was all but banned. Everything was nationalized. Everything had to belong to the state.

In normal countries, private ownership is sacred. In the Soviet Union, private ownership was, to put it mildly, frowned upon. In reality, it only existed in a very limited form.

My maternal great grandparents—my mother's grandmom and granddad—lived in an apartment in a house that used to belong to someone else. The previous owners had three buildings before the commies came in, and all the three buildings were nationalized. They managed to buy back their own house, the place they had actually lived.

The two buildings that had also been in their possession were taken away from them and converted into apartment buildings—even if they had space for two apartments only. The state had the control.

The house in which my great grandparents had a studio apartment, the lower floor used to be a store, and there were two apartments in the upper floor. The store was long gone, it was empty, unused, neglected, nobody gave two shits about that space.

The two apartments on the second floor—one inhabited by my great grandparents and the other by an odd Russian couple—consisting of a mom and a daughter who constantly fought, to the extent of the daughter punching the lights out of her mother—were the dwelling places for human beings.

I guess my great grandparents were happy in that teeny-tiny apartment, even though they had to hear their neighbors fight all the time. At one point, the Russians next door to them got physical. The daughter jawed her mother so badly that, as my great grandmother put it, "Her mouth was full of blood."

The fuck's wrong with these people, I thought.

Then again, violence was all around us. It seemed as if we couldn't live without it. We couldn't strive without it. Moreover, we couldn't even survive without it.

My maternal grandmother—the daughter of my great grandparents—once told me how she one time, when she was young, returned home after the curfew. "My father raised his hand as if he was going to hit me. He never did," she confided in me. But the entire thought of hitting one's daughter, that must've been a generational thing. Or maybe he was just mean?

I decided I would never hit a woman. I found that awful. If I had a daughter, hitting her would be even worse, I thought.

2

I was always fascinated with cars. Ever since I could remember. And my great grandparents' neighbors—the ones who had bought back their own house from the Soviet occupiers, the ones in whose former house my great grandparents lived in—always worked on their cars in their courtyard.

"I'm going to give you a beating if you go over there," my great grandfather said when I went out to the garden. I always played in the garden.

And, sure as shit, I walked over to the neighbors' garage where they worked on a car.

And my great grandfather came to get me—even though I wasn't disturbing the neighbors. It seemed like they liked me coming over, the fact I was interested, the fact that I wanted to learn about cars, about what they were doing.

My great grandfather dragged me away from there.

"I told you not to go there. Now you're going to get a beating."

He didn't give me one, though. He took me to the shed and gave me a lecture. About how his word was what mattered and that whatever I wanted to do, didn't. I was maybe five years old. Maybe six. I thought what I wanted mattered, too. Evidently, it didn't.

But he never, ever raised a hand against me, even if he had threatened to do so.

He was a good guy. He taught me a lot.

3

That house on Gutter Street in Tallinn, that was where I grew up. We lived in a small, three-hundred-and-sixty-six-square-foot apartment on the first floor. We had a bedroom, we had a living room, we had a kitchen. And there was a basement box for all our shit that needed storage. We kept our winter potatoes in there, some jams and other preserves that our relatives in the countryside had made, but the most space was taken up by peat briquettes we used for heating.

There was an old-fashioned stove in the kitchen that my mom used for heating and cooking. There was also a natural gas stove, but that was for summer cooking. In the winter, you needed to use the stove and if you're already using the stove for heating, you may just as well cook on it, to save money on gas.

And in my parents' bedroom, there was a furnace. Mom and dad heated the furnace up by burning wood and peat briquettes and that was to provide heat for the entire apartment. It did. But every now and then, I'd wake up and be freezing. The fire had all burned up; my parents were sleeping, and I would be cold. It was not their fault. It was the fault of the system.

To be honest, it could've been worse. According to the stories, when I was born, my parents lived in a single room in a two-room apartment in a bedroom community. These communities that were built by the Soviets after World War Two around Tallinn had eight to sixteen-story buildings with apartments with tiny bedrooms and kitchens and many of these apartments housed multiple families.

After I was born, they applied for their own apartment. This was how it was done in the Soviet Union—there was no selling and buying of living spaces. You had to apply for a bigger apartment. Or you had to cheat.

They did that, too. Later. But at this point, after spending years in the line, they managed to snatch this small, three-hundred-and-sixty-six-foot apartment.

I'm sure I was happier there than I would have been in the said bedroom community, living out of one room together with my parents. But was my childhood happy?

Later in my childhood, I got a part in a movie that was directed by the former boyfriend of my mother. The movie was set in the 1950s, during the Stalinist purge of the undesirables, and how the children lived during this time. It was a great movie, and it was called, "A Happy Childhood." The premise of the movie was: however shitty things were, the kids were always happy, the kids always enjoyed a happy childhood.

Well, fuck me blue. I was born in 1979. The Stalinist purges were long gone. The life in the Soviet Union was close to normal—at least the normal we'd know. And I cannot say my life was anything close to happy.

4

I went to the kindergarten for two days. I don't remember absolutely anything about those two days.

But I do know that it's probably not the best idea to send a sociopath to the kindergarten. At a later age, a sociopath learns to manage his contempt for other people. You learn to play nice, or not so nice, but at least you learn to play. When you're three or four years old, you don't have the ability to learn the proper human interaction.

I've always been repulsed by people. Well, most people. I never had too many friends. Not many people could handle me; I couldn't handle many people. I was a lonely kid, but it kind of suited me. It was better to play alone than handle other people's wants, needs, and feelings.

Animals were much better companions than people, I thought. I begged my parents for a dog. I wanted a rough collie. Like Lassie. I never got one.

***

I was raised by my great grandmother and great grandfather—the same ones who lived in the house that used to belong to someone else.

They lived on the other side of the town. Every workday morning, my dad and I got on a bus, then changed the bus, and then walked to get to my great grandparents' house. And then my dad would take the same buses back to his office. The commute was a pain for me. I couldn't have imagined what pain it was for him—but, being a kid, I didn't give that part much of a thought.

I hated riding buses. Steering them was another story; riding them was such a hassle. They were slow, they were loud, they pushed out atrociously dark and stinky fumes. They were all yellow and came from Hungary. They kept stopping at bus stops to let other people in and out. Not fair, I thought, I was already on the bus.

It took about an hour to get from my home to my great grandparents' house. It took my dad another hour to get to his office. Then, in the evening, either he or my mom would come and pick me up. Again, riding the two buses for an hour there and an hour back.

I probably didn't appreciate their efforts; I was too young to understand.

***

My great grandparents had had a very hard life. Both had survived two world wars. They had lived in eastern Estonia, in a border town called Narva. Close to the end of World War II, the approaching Soviet forces bombed Narva to oblivion. They didn't have any other option than to evacuate. So, they took their earthly possessions—of which they had very few—put them on a cart and, pushing and pulling the cart, they walked 130 miles to Tallinn, the capital.

As did the rest of the residents of the town. The Soviet authorities later resettled Narva with ethnic Russians, moved in from elsewhere in the Soviet Union, making sure the Estonian border town would forever become a Russian one. It is one to this day; even though within the Estonian borders, its majority population is ethnic Russians of whom not all view living in an independent Estonia such a treat after all.

After the Soviets occupied Estonia, they imposed their communist rule, nationalized all private property, and gave my great grandparents a studio apartment in a house that used to belong to someone else. They settled there and lived out their lives. They had a beautiful garden with apple trees, berry bushes, flowers that they tended to.

***

My great grandfather was eighty years old when his daughter—my grandmother—and her husband got a plot in the countryside for a summer cottage. At eighty years old, my great grandfather started to build the cottage. He did most of the construction work. At EIGHTY.

The humankind doesn't produce men like these old-timers were—not anymore. I don't even know if I live until eighty, let alone be fit enough to build a log cottage and an attached sauna.

5

I filled my days at my great grandparents' place with playing in the garden. But I did some work, too. My great grandfather taught me to saw wood— they, too, had a wood-burning stove that provided heat and a cooktop.

He didn't let me chop wood, though, because "the axe isn't a toy," as he said. I wasn't allowed to touch the axe until I was older because all grownups were worried I'd chop my own legs off. I didn't know if that was a legitimate concern, but then again, my brother managed to hit his own leg with an axe when he was in his thirties. Maybe it was a legitimate concern after all.

The house didn't have flowing water. There was a deep well about a hundred yards from it, and my great grandfather walked to it many times a day with a bucket or two to get water. It was the freshest water I had ever tasted. But imagine, being in your mid-eighties, walking with two three-gallon buckets to the well and back many times a day.

He taught me to lift the water out of the well. But I wasn't strong enough to carry the buckets. Not until I was older.

There were no kids my age—or otherwise—in the neighborhood. Or maybe there were, I just didn't meet them. I was strictly forbidden to leave the garden unless I was sent on a chore. Like going to the store about half a mile away to get the groceries.

One day I was sent to get some milk and eggs. All my ancestors—my parents, my grandparents and my great grandparents—always gave me the exact sum of money needed for the groceries I was supposed to get, to the penny. All prices were standardized in the Soviet Union, everyone knew how much something cost.

I walked to the store, got the necessary groceries and was ready to pay at the register when the cashier informed of a significant development.

"We've just been delivered bananas," she told me. "Go tell your parents."

I had heard about bananas. I knew what they looked like. Yellow, curvy. Were supposed to taste really well. But I had never seen one. Let alone tasted one.

I ran back to my great grandparents' house.

"They just told me at the store they had bananas delivered!" I told them, but without any real excitement—I didn't know what to be excited about. And I didn't really want to spend their money—poor pensioners who didn't have much of it anyway. But the lady at the store had told me to tell my parents. The closest thing to my parents present were my great grandparents.

Besides, I thought they would be more excited about something so rare as bananas than I was—especially because they knew what they were, and I only guessed.

They weren't too excited. But they gave me some money for a couple of bananas. I ran back to the store, got a few and walked back, again not being very excited. The only reason I had run was because I was afraid they'd run out and I couldn't bring my great grandfolks the bananas that had been promised.

That day I had the first banana of my life. I was six years old.

6

When I was about four years old, my parents took me on my first trip "abroad." Well, it wasn't exactly abroad as Estonia was occupied by the Soviet Union and the entire Soviet Union was supposed to be my homeland to love and cherish.

We took an airplane—an old Tupolev 134 that shook and rattled like a wooden roller coaster at a nineteenth-century county fair—to Moscow, the capital of Russia and the entire Soviet Union. I'd like to think that the traveling we do is supposed to teach us something. And when our parents take us on travels, they want to teach us something.

I have no idea what I was supposed to learn in Moscow. Sure, we saw the Kremlin, the Red Square, the Russian Orthodox churches, the lot. And we spent the best part of a day standing in a line to see a mummy.

Vladimir Ilyich fucking Lenin. The great founder of the Soviet fucking Union. The fuckhead responsible of the murder of millions. The god-awful bastard responsible for bringing misery to hundreds of millions. The dipshit responsible for the monstrosity the Soviet Union was.

His supposed body lay in the mausoleum, right by the Kremlin, on the Red Square. And evidently it was part of every young communist soldier's rite of passage to stand in line over half a day to see that rotten and still rotting corpse that no one was even sure was him.

Lenin had died in 1924. Now sure, the ancient Egyptians possessed the skills of mummifying bodies that would withstand millennia. The Russians of 1924, unfortunately, didn't. The Russians of any year of the Soviet Union—and before and after it—had never produced, created, or made anything that would last, would stand the test of time, would be workable.

So that was the suspicion about Lenin—that his actual body had been buried a long time ago and what lay in the mausoleum was just a doll, made of plastic, or pure cow shit for that matter.

Nevertheless, my parents—especially my dad who was a communist party apparatchik—insisted we stood in the line, in a not particularly pleasant weather, to see the man who had wanted to create a communist utopia that never was. There we were, standing in that slow-moving line, hoping to see a supposed corpse.

The supposed corpse was white. It was just like a tiny old guy, laying in a coffin with a glass cover. Unimpressionable, boring, just a thing without meaning.

And yet, thousands of people spent hours every day standing in the line, in shitty weather, to see that thing. It was as if they absolutely had to do it.

***

From Moscow, we flew to Crimea, a peninsula in Ukraine, right in the Black Sea. The plane this time around was an Ilyushin 86, a bigger old aircraft that shook and rattled like a wooden roller coaster at a nineteenth-century county fair.

That was supposed to be a beach vacation. Nothing to learn, just lay back, relax and enjoy the sea.

That it, indeed, was. Apart from the day we took a trip on a hydrofoil boat. In a true Soviet fashion, the boat was built so badly that I got seasick on calm waters. This was my first memory of puking my guts out so badly that when I ran out of stomach contents, just pure bile came out and it seemed never to end.

Later, when I was a tad older, it would happen many times. Hangovers can be a bitch.

7

When we flew back from Crimea to Moscow, it turned out our return flight from Moscow to Tallinn had been canceled. We had to take the train.

If you think airplanes in the Soviet Union were a horrendous experience, imagine spending 14 hours in a train car with bus seats that you can't push back. And then imagine being four years old and having to spend a night on a bus seat, trying to catch some sleep while the seat keeps jumping up and down along with the rails.

At least there was an endless supply of tea. There was a stewardess in every car whose sole job was to give you tea every time you asked. Tea in Russia was actually good, but how much of it can you consume?

Another problem was using the restroom. The way the Soviet long-distance trains' restrooms were built was, everything that came out of your body landed straight on the tracks. No septic tanks, just a pipe from the rusty, disgusting aluminum toilet bowl straight down to the tracks. You weren't allowed to use the shitter at train stations, only when the train was moving could you pee and shit. Or puke, if that was your affliction.

The amount of shit on the train tracks in the Soviet Union must have pushed the earth out of its tilt and caused global warming. And here we are, blaming cows.

In the morning, not far from Tallinn, I was extremely hungry. There was a restaurant car, so I begged my parents to get us some food.

"You don't want that blue baked chicken," my dad told me.

"Why is it blue?" I asked.

"Because it's gone bad. And they don't serve anything else here."

I was miserable. There was no food, only the endless supply of tea. I didn't believe "blue chicken" would be bad for me.

And I was angry at my parents for not feeding me—I thought it was because they didn't want to spend money on the expensive train chow.

In the long run, though, I think it was a good thing I didn't eat rotten chicken.

8

It was in November of 1984 when my mother suddenly went to the hospital. I knew what to expect. She had been pregnant for a long time—at the time, I didn't know how babies were even born or conceived. When I asked, my parents would tell me, "If two people love each other very much, babies are born."

That was good enough for me.

I was at my grandmother's and her husband's—I called him pop-pops— place when the news came.

"You have a little brother," they told me. I must have missed something, because I exclaimed, "A sister!"

"No-no, a brother," they reiterated. Oh, a brother. Same difference. I was excited to have a sibling.

Back in these deep, dark Soviet times, fathers weren't allowed to accompany their wives' giving birth. The women were secluded in a birthing hospital, and after they had given birth, they could only wave to their husbands who were eagerly waiting on the street in front of the hospital. The women would wave their babies in front of the windows and the men down at the streets would applaud and wait until their wives were signed out of the hospital so that they could take their babies home.

We took a cab to the hospital. Taking a taxi was a big thing back then. It cost outrageous money, and there were no cabs available. People would stand in lines at taxi stands, sometimes for hours, to catch the next available cab to pull up.

My mom walked out, carrying my teeny-tiny little brother, wrapped in blankets and towels, and we sat in the taxi and the cabbie drove us home.

I had a little brother. I didn't realize that little shit would take ALL attention away from me. Suddenly, I was a nobody. All the attention went to him. "Look how cute he is!" "We need to change his diaper!" "We need to feed him!" Jesus fuck. What about me?

They named him Danny. I used to torture him. Maybe because I was a sociopath. Maybe because I was tortured on a daily basis in school, so I needed an outlet to torture someone else, someone weaker than me. We spent years fighting each other. It took both of us growing up for me to realize, he wasn't only my brother. He was actually my bro.

I don't think I trust anyone more than my brother. Now. And now I'm ashamed of what a little shit I was to him all the years we grew up together.

Yes, it turns out I was the little shit, not him, and all he tried to do was to grow up in a safe, normal environment, and I may have deprived him of that.

It's not easy to be a sociopath.

9

My family wasn't exactly poor. Well, depends on the standards. We weren't poor according to the standards of the Soviet Union. We were dirt poor compared with anyone living in the West. The good thing about it was, we didn't know any better.

My father was a communist party apparatchik, not very well off, but did fine. He worked many jobs throughout my childhood. He used to go to the office every workday by nine o'clock and returned home after the workday had concluded at six o'clock in the evening.

My mother was a tailor. She used to sow clothes for her friends, sometimes strangers. Clothes were hard to come by these days—much like anything else—and she provided a service everyone could use. She bought yards and yards of different cloths and sew pants, shirts, dresses, coats, whatnot, out of it. She provided a valuable service and her customers appreciated that.

But we lived in that three-hundred-and-sixty-six-square-foot one-bedroom apartment on Gutter Street. My mother, my father, my brother, and me. And, at times, my great grandmother. The apartment was too small for two people, let alone for five. We had to manage.

It was the fault of the system. Since there was almost no private property, there was no buying or selling real estate. There were no mortgages, there was no "if I work harder, I can afford a better place." That didn't exist and we didn't even know life could be any different.

We didn't have a car. In order to buy a new car in the Soviet Union, you needed to get a permit to buy a car. And those permits were scarce. Only the people with really high-end jobs—or people who had high-end connections—got those.

And cars were ridiculously expensive. There was no system of making monthly car payments. You waited in the line for the car buying permit for ten years and, at the same time, collected money to buy one. There was no second-hand car market, not really. Whoever got their hands onto a car, kept it for life. Every car owner was a qualified mechanic, too. Or they had to know someone who was.

Both of my grandfathers had cars. My maternal grandfather had the cheapest, the shittiest, the most horrendous car ever. It was called Zaporozhets. It was the lowest end of the Soviet-manufactured cars, with the engine in the rear and no cooling system—it was air-cooled.

My paternal grandfather had a Lada 2106. That was a very high-end "people's car." A small piece-of-shit vehicle, but if you had the oh-six, as it was called, you were the king. He worked in a factory that produced bricks, and that factory supplied the entire Soviet Union with them. He was a higher-up, and he got a permit to buy a car. And he indeed bought a car.

The average salary in my circle of people was around two hundred rubles a month. A pensioner could get as little as fifty rubles from the state a month. I have no idea how much my grandfather with the 2106 made, but it couldn't have been a lot more than the average.

His car cost ten thousand rubles. He was the king.

Later, when car buying got a little easier, my dad bought a car. It was a Zaporozhets, similar to what my mother's dad had. It constantly broke down and my granddad worked on it because he was a specialist in repairing Zaporozhets vehicles.

I learned a lot from him. I can fix BMWs today because I learned how to fix the shittiest cars on earth when I was a teenager. I can't say growing up in the Soviet Union never taught me anything.

10

I can't think of a worse day than the first day of school.

At the end of the day, they told me I had to go back. For the next twelve years. ARE YOU FUCKING KIDDING ME, I wanted to yell. I may have, too.

I was always the little fat kid. I wasn't necessarily obese, but I was chubby enough. What do you get if you eat shit all day and don't exercise, eh?

I hated exercise. I still do, but now, as an old man, I do it anyway. I have to. I want to live longer, I love life, so I exercise. Back then, though, I didn't. Exercising was my worst nightmare.

But that wasn't why I hated school. I started school in September 1985. The Soviet Union was still going strong. I hated school because all the teachers were from the 1500s. Their education had been as standardized as our education was. Their education was based on ancient teaching systems that shouldn't have been conceived in the first place.

And yet they were.

We had two types of exercise books at the time. One was lined vertically for writing, the other one as lined vertically and horizontally for doing math. And we had to draw sidelines or edge lines or whatnot, I don't even know what the fuck to call them. Basically, the sideline had to be five squares from the outer edge and two squares from the inner edge.

But I didn't know how that worked. I was six years old. My dad had always taken care of the sidelines.

Maybe it was because I was six years old—I had started school a year earlier than anybody else. My parents were adamant that I was a genius, so I needed to start school a year earlier than everyone else.

I wasn't a fucking genius. I was an average student. And they—my parents—exposed me to a world of shit. I never appreciated that.

One day, the class teacher gave us sheets of squared paper and told us to draw the sidelines. I didn't know what they were. She said, five squares from the outer edge and two squares from the inner edge.

So that's what I drew. I went five squares down from the outer edge and two squares down from the inner edge.

The bell rang. Everyone walked outside. I had nowhere to go.

The class teacher walked to me and saw what I had drawn.

"Are these sidelines?" she screamed from the top of her lungs, and then shoved the piece of paper in my face. There I was, a six-year-old boy, getting a piece of paper shoved up in my face by a more righteous-than-thou teacher who had no business of being a teacher in the first place.

I was told to stand in the corner of the classroom. Standing in the corner until your shame passes was a standard punishment in the Soviet Union. But a teacher humiliating a student for something he didn't know he was doing wrong, that was even beyond my imagination.

She broke my nose. I was bleeding. "Go to the bathroom, put some cold water on it," she advised me.

Go fuck yourself, you bitch, I wanted to tell her. But I was six years old. I would've been really ballsy, had I done it.

I wasn't that ballsy. And I didn't yet know the necessary words. I'd learn them soon.

And there I was, standing in the corner with by bleeding nose and crushed pride, thinking that how can it be this bitch got to be a teacher at all.

This bitch should be stoned, I thought, and then changed my mind. She should be stoned, resurrected, and then stoned again, I thought.

11

My school was actually very close to our house, but there were big factories around us, so I had to walk around them. Every workday, I got up at six thirty in the morning, brushed my teeth, washed my face, ate some horrendous hot cereal that I hated, and walked fifteen minutes to school—that I hated even more.

In those days, we all had to wear a uniform to school. It was a blue one with a white shirt. The boys had a blue jacket and blue pants, while the girls had a blue dress—and no jacket. On top of that military-style idiocy, we had a cap. The good thing was, wearing the cap was optional.

As I've said, the Soviet Union was a standardized country—everything was set in stone, everyone had to behave according to the same unvarying and unwavering rules and regulations.

And there we were—Lenin's little soldiers, dressed accordingly, every day ready to learn how the world's proletarians needed to unite to build a better, communist future for us all.

It could have been worse. In the past, kids in the Soviet Union had gone to school six days a week. I guess that's something.

My walk to school was usually peaceful. Our street—Gutter Street—was lined with lime trees that in the spring would blossom and smell really well, and in the fall would drop their colorful leaves at my footsteps.

In the summer, they would leave sap everywhere, but, thankfully, there was no school in the summer.

My walk back from the school, oftentimes, wasn't as peaceful. Sometimes I had to run away from the bullies. Sometimes they caught me. Sometimes they didn't.

My entire aim was to run to somewhere where there were other adults around, so that the bullies wouldn't dare to beat me up or torture me otherwise.

Most of the time, there were some adults around. Some of the time, the grown-ups actually gave a shit or two about the little fat kid who was about to get his ass kicked by bigger, stronger boys, and I could feel safe again.

12

The way Estonians make friends is, they go to the first grade, the sit down at their assigned desks, and they see their desk mates. They introduce themselves, and they stay friends for life. Moreover, that's when the friend-making process ends. Never, later in their lives, would most Estonians make any friends, or at least not friends as dear as their first desk mates.

In first grade, I made two friends. I guess I was the lucky one. One was Simon, the other was Michael. I was closer to Simon because he lived a fifteen-minute walk from me. Michael lived in the same borough my great grandparents did, so it was a lot harder to commute to his place.

The rest of the kids hated me. And I hated them.

During the Soviet times, the school was managed like the military. We had to go to class, which lasted forty-five minutes, then we had five to fifteen-minute breaks, depending on the time of the day, and then by one or two o'clock in the afternoon, it was over. We all went home, did our homework, and then we were free to do whatever the fuck else we wanted.

School started at quarter to eight. Seven-forty-five. I couldn't grasp how the adults always went to work by nine o'clock in the morning, but children—who needed their beauty sleeps—had to get to class by seven fucking forty-five.

But it was what it was.

During the breaks between classes, we were only allowed to walk in circles. No matter how long the break was, we were allowed to stay in groups of two or three and just walk around the hallway in circles.

There was an old teacher—a high-school chemistry teacher—who guarded the floor we were at. He had a long wooden stick and he walked in the middle of the hallway, and he yelled at anyone who fell out of line.

No running. No talking. Just walking around the hallway.

***

There were two girls I liked. Janice and Marcia. They were in the same class I was. I always made my business to walk near them. We sometimes whispered things to each other, even though it wasn't allowed.

"You're my girlfriend," I whispered Marcia.

"You're my girlfriend," I whispered to Janice.

They were walking together, and they both, of course, heard what I had whispered to each of them.

Hell, I didn't know any better. I should've known you can't confess your love to two different girls at the same time while they're both hearing you.

They didn't know better, either. Fortunately for me. They were flattered. They didn't have any problem with being the girlfriends of one guy, let alone a guy who was so awkward and sociopathic that he didn't have any business of getting a single girl, let alone two.

And I wouldn't have known what to do with a girl anyway, let alone two.

They sure were pretty. I loved them.

13

One day, my classmate Troy had a playing card with him. It was a seven of diamonds. Maybe a seven of hearts. It was definitely a seven.

In the middle of the card, there was a cock. And a pretty, blonde woman sucking it. It was the first depiction of pornography I ever saw.

Troy went around the class, showing it to all the boys. We had a field day. There it was, a woman giving a blowjob. Pornography was banned in the Soviet Union. We had seen something illegal AND cool.

There was this old Soviet joke. A guy walks home from a bar when suddenly someone approaches him from a dark alley. "Hey, you wanna buy some pornography?" the guy from the alley asks. The guy walking home replies, "Hell, no. I don't even have a pornographer."

That's how alien it was to us.

I told Janice and Marcia about the picture. "Did you see the picture Troy had?" I asked them. Marcia replied resolutely, "Only sick people look at pictures like that."

They stopped being my girlfriends that moment. Not because I stopped liking them. They stopped liking me because I was sick. I had looked at a picture of a blowjob.

And I didn't even know it was a blowjob and why I was sick for looking at it.

14

I learned to jerk off at an early age. I don't even know where I learned it from because porn was alien to me, I hadn't seen or heard anything about what people did in their bedrooms other than sleep. And I certainly didn't know that touching your dick in a certain way would bring you pleasure.

And yet, I did know. Intuitively, perhaps? I don't know.

What I did know was, when you stroke your cock enough times, you'd feel so fucking good. It was an out of this world feeling that nothing could replace. Not even excessive eating.

And when I had learned to jerk off, I did it every chance I got. And I did know that this was something you do privately. Maybe I knew because I had to take my dick out of my pants, and you don't take your dick out of your pants when someone might see you. That's just something you don't do.

I did get caught, though. My mother walked in on my when I was just starting, and even though I put it away the moment she walked in, she knew what I had been doing.

"Only stupid men do that," she told me. "Don't ever do that again!"

I promised I wouldn't.

It turned out I lied.

But that was the extent of sexual education in the Soviet Union. We didn't learn about sex from our parents, let alone in school. We learned about it from our friends who had learned about it from their friends. And in theory we were all strong; in practice, we didn't know shit.

"There's no sex in the USSR," a journalist once exclaimed on live TV. That was probably the reason there was no sexual education in the USSR, either.

The USSR stood for the Union of Soviet Socialist Republics. That was its official name. Everyone called it by its nickname—the Soviet Union.

One summer I was at my paternal grandmother's and grandfather's place in the tiny village they lived at. I had figured out that I could climb under a sofa and be alone there. And soon I figured out that if I'm alone there, I can jerk off there in peace.

That went on for a while, until my grandmother noticed I spent lengthy amounts of time under the sofa. And one time, sure as shit, she leaned down to look at what I was doing and almost caught me with my dick in my hand. I had managed to put it away just a microsecond before her line of sight reached underneath the sofa—yet, she knew.

"You were playing with your pee-pee," she said.

"No, I wasn't."

"Yes, you were."

"No, I wasn't."

My oldest cousin, Roderick—somewhat a bully at that age—was there, too. "Yes, you were playing with your pee-pee," he reiterated, even though he hadn't seen me.

That pissed me off.

"No, I wasn't," I shot back.

"Yes, you were," Roderick said, as if he knew for certain.

But that was the end of it. I don't know if my grandmother ever told my grandfather or my parents, but I did have the feeling that if she told my grandfather, he calmed her down and told her to not to tell my parents.

I was fairly sure my grandfather jerked off all the time.

15

The hierarchy was in place. If you wanted to be cool, you had to hang around the cool kids. You had to be lean, mean, a cool machine to be accepted in the cool kids' hierarchy.

My friend Simon was that. My friend Michael was that, too. He could run really fucking fast and that impressed everyone.

I wasn't lean, mean, nor a cool machine.

I don't actually know why Simon was my friend. Was it the vicinity of our abodes? I don't know. We were too young to analyze things.

I was the little fat kid most of my elementary school life. I was too lazy and too fat to play any sports—and I didn't even want to. I hated exercise. I hated the physical education classes. They made us to squats, push-ups, pull-ups, climb the rope, play basketball, play soccer. For all I cared, they could have made us suck each other's cocks; I wanted no part of it.

Simon was a sports guy. He made friends easily with other sports guys.

Too bad those other guys were bullies and regular average assholes.

There was Conrad, who, not surprisingly, in his adult life became a dentist. Give a sadist the option to choose their career and they will choose the most sadistic of them all.

There was John, who didn't become anything. He exhausted all his bullying during elementary school but didn't find time to actually learn anything and thus became nothing.

There was Peter, who became a real estate mogul. He's the only one of my former bullies who actually, later in my life, became my friend. But back in school, he was a proper asshole. Once, he kicked me in the face with his foot.

I had his sole marks on my face for a week.

And Simon was friends with them all. Whenever they were together, he wasn't my friend. He was my bully. He had this strong desire to fit in with the bullies that he forgot he was my friend.

I didn't blame him for that. Fitting in was important. It was my fault that I didn't.

One time, I was taking a bus home and Simon, Conrad and John were riding their bikes and they saw me. They all wanted to torture me some more, so they chased the bus as far as they could, but soon fell back. The bus driver saw that I was escaping from a bunch of assholes, so he asked me where I was going. The house where my apartment was between two bus stops. He stopped in front of my house to let me out so that I could run inside.

When the bullies saw I had gotten out of the bus, they raced their bikes towards me, hoping they'd catch me before I had the chance to run into the house. Fortunately, I made it. I got into the house right before they pedaled their way there. They circled around the house, whistling and calling me names, but they hadn't caught me. Simon was among these assholes.

***

And yet, Simon was a gentle soul. Whenever we were together, alone, apart from the gang of bullies, he was the sweetest guy. I could see he cherished my friendship as I cherished his.

He surely understood that me being his friend was more beneficial to me than to him. I had a place to go, to escape my parents and the apartment, to go to another reality, to play different games, to relate to different people than the ones around me every day.

But he also understood that him being my friend connected him to normality. He wasn't a bully at heart. He just wanted to fit in with the gang of bullies and he couldn't help it. He played the role of a bully when he was with the bullies, but he was nice, kind, loving when we were alone.

Simon lived with his dad, uncle and grandmother in a big house about half a mile from me. He also had a mother whom I met once. She was a blonde lady living somewhere else, with someone else. I never asked him what had happened between his dad and mom, or how he ended up living with his dad rather than his mother.

But I heard stories. Simon's mother drank. A lot. Of course, Simon's father drank, too, and by the looks of it, far more than his mother. Simon's uncle drank, too, a little less than his father.

Simon's grandma didn't drink. It was her job to take care of both of her sons and her grandson. Plus, the two dogs who were more vicious than a hungry mountain lion in a lifeless desert. She had a hard life.

But she cooked great home-made food that I seemed to appreciate more than Simon.

Simon was the one who taught me to smoke and drink. I'm eternally grateful to him.

16

I had never been good with pain. Be it with receiving torture from my classmates, getting the belt from the elderly—which I was really spared from—or getting medical treatment that involved inducing pain.

But it turned out I hadn't experienced real pain until my dad took me to what turned out to be the worst place in the known universe.

The dentist's office.

The dentist's office was in the same clinic our general practitioner worked at. Actually, just two doors down from her. It was the children's wing, so I thought all the children's doctors were close to each other so they could exchange notes.

I didn't know what to expect. I had never been to the dentist before.

The dentist was a young-ish woman who invited me and my dad into her office and led me to the dentist's chair that looked creepy enough. It wasn't a regular chair where you sit up; they put you in an unnatural, almost like a fetal position, and then shove a light in your face.

"Don't worry about anything, it's not going to hurt," the dentist said.

And I made the mistake of believing her.

At first, she poked around my teeth with some really sharp, pokey instruments. It didn't hurt, but I was very uncomfortable.

If I had only known what would come next.

She took out a drill. And started drilling my teeth. With a fucking drill. That was the size of my thumb.

The Soviet Union was a fucked-up country. It was so fucked up that it didn't have dental anesthesia. Everyone had their teeth drilled without any numbness.

My dad may have actually enjoyed that. Later in life, when dental anesthesia was already available—for a separate fee—he would forgo it and endure the full pain of drilling his teeth. He would say the occasional "aah" here and here from the pain, but it didn't seem to bother him enough to fork out the few units of money to get the anesthesia.

I wasn't even given that option.

I screamed. I shook my head. I did everything I possibly could to keep that fucking drill out of my mouth.

My dad had to step in and hold my head still. He used all his strength to do that, and the dentist used all of hers to keep my mouth open so that she could drill the many, many cavities I had developed.

And I kept screaming. And biting the dentist's fingers. She was a real fucking sadist, and biting her fingers was the only way I could think of to get her out of my fucking mouth. I wish I had had the strength to bite some of her fingers off.

It was the worst pain of pains I could've imagined. Or couldn't even imagine altogether. Even purgatory—or hell itself for that matter—would have been less painful, had I only known about them.

The dentist shoved all my cavities with silver amalgam fillings. Nothing else was available in the Soviet Union. My mouth was full of heavy metal. But not the good kind of heavy metal.

My mouth hurt like hell for a week.

***

My school also had a dentist's office. Every once in a while, some kids had to go there, to get their mandatory dental checks done. They tortured the kids there, too, like the dentist had tortured me.

The Soviet Union took special pleasure in torturing people.

Whenever it looked like they were going to call me to the school's dentist, I would just fuck the fuck off. I'd just skip school. No way I wanted to experience this trauma again.

I didn't go to the dentist for over ten years after that first experience.

17

Whenever we had parties—mostly birthdays of various people—we'd all sit at a long table. Sometimes, when the room wasn't big enough, the kids had their own separate table in a different room. So that they couldn't listen in to adult conversations, but mostly that the adults would be left alone with whatever they had to talk about, and the kids could play among themselves.

The tables at my paternal grandparents' and my maternal grandparents' apartments were usually the longest, and there, most of the time, the kids would sit at the adults' table. But my aunts' apartments were smaller, so often, the long tables there didn't have any space for kids. They were put somewhere else. Kids weren't considered human. "A kid speaks when a chicken pees," was common knowledge, told to me by almost every adult I met.

But I knew chickens didn't pee. They just defecate everything.

The adults drank vodka. There wasn't anything else around, really. Well, there were liqueurs, there was beer, there was horrendously shitty wine, but at a party, everyone drank vodka.

Gets you drunk the quickest, I thought.

The good thing about guests is, they eventually leave. And when they leave, the kids are normally asked to bring all the dishes to the kitchen, to clean all the shit up the grownups left behind.

But all the shot glasses had droplets of vodka left. My job—one that I had assigned myself to—was to go through all the shot glasses and empty them into my stomach.

Ugh. Vodka tasted dreadfully. But the curiosity, the need to understand why the grownups drank and—most importantly—why the kids weren't given any, always had the best of me. So, every time there was a party, anywhere, and every time no one noticed, I'd go around the table and drink all the droplets that were left behind in the shot glasses.

And after that, I'd either feel really well, or I'd puke my guts out. It was about a fifty-sixty chance of either happening.

My dad would occasionally give me beer foam when he was having a drink outside of a party. Drinking beer in the evening was normal, it just wasn't offered in parties. Whenever I heard the sound of a beer cork coming off a bottle, I'd be there, just to taste foam.

Maybe I was programmed to be an alcoholic from an early age. But that's not my parents' fault.

18

Simon's friend Devon lived not far from his house. He was an older gentleman, about ten years older than we were. But he liked us boys going over there, he liked to entertain us and get us things we couldn't get ourselves—like cigarettes or booze. Devon seemed like a good guy.

"Let's go over to Devon's," Simon proposed one day.

"Who's Devon?" I asked.

"Just a friend. He can get us smokes and drinks, he's old enough."

Fine by me. My dad had smoked as long as I had known him, so I thought no harm there.

Actually, there had been harm. I once took a burning cigarette from an ashtray and took a puff. It was a cigarette of a family friend. Shortly after, I developed stomatitis, a nasty infection of gums that included blisters all around my mouth. I went to the doctor for weeks and got ointment for my mouth.

"It's because of smoking," my mom told me. And I believed her. I thought that puff was the cause of the blisters in my mouth. Of course, it wasn't. She lied to me to keep me away from cigarettes.

That didn't work.

So we went to Devon's house. He lived by the railroad depot with his mother, but he had a den where he could host us and bring us cigarettes and booze.

He sure as shit got us cigarettes and booze. And so we sat there, I learned to smoke and drink, but I only had a few sips of the beer he got. I smoked half a pack of cigarettes.

I puked my guts out after that. But for some reason, that didn't hinder my desire to smoke, either. I wanted to be a grownup and smoke like the grownups did.

Everyone around me smoked. I wanted to smoke, too.

Smoking tobacco was fun. For years to come, I was able to manage it. When I was in the sight of my parents or anyone else who would frown upon me smoking, I was able to refrain from it. I didn't need to smoke. I wasn't addicted.

Until one point when I realized I was. And I couldn't stop.

***

Some time later Simon told me he wouldn't go back to Devon's house. He had learned Devon was a bit of a pedophile.

"He won't stick his hand down your pants if you don't want it," Simon said.

I didn't want it. I guess Simon didn't want it, either.

19

Smoking cigarettes throughout my teenage life was a burden. I couldn't do it publicly—none of us could, and all of us smoked—so it meant constant sneaking around, constant hiding.

One time, Simon, Michael, and I had scored a pack of Polish filterless cigarettes. We smoked in the woods not far from my house and somehow, I ended up with the pack. Thank god I was wise enough to hide the pack before I went home.

"Have you been smoking?" my mom yelled at me. She had smelled it in my breath. I was wise enough to hide the pack, but I was dumb enough to not know your breath stinks after you've smoked.

"No, mom," I lied.

"I can smell it on you!"

"I haven't smoked!"

"Let's see where you hid the cigarettes." She searched me from head to toe, and then said, "Maybe you put them somewhere else."

She walked to the basement, turned over all the obvious places. No cigarettes there. She walked to the back garden. Looked around, but fortunately not too thoroughly. The pack was right by the back door, hidden in the grass so it wouldn't be visible to the naked eye.

I dodged a massive bullet. I have no idea what my parents might have done to me if they had found conclusive proof that I was smoking. Kids weren't supposed to smoke. Kids were supposed to be punished when they did shit the grown-ups were fine to do.

And even though almost everyone around us smoked, what our parents and grandparents taught us was, "If you smoke, your growth will stall." We didn't care about that; we didn't believe it.

We all grew up to be taller than our parents. Maybe they smoked when they were kids, too.

***

What is it about smoking that gives us so much pleasure? I don't know. I do know that it did give me pleasure to the extent of never wanting to quit.

My dad smoked. He didn't smoke in the apartment; he went to the hallway to smoke. When he had friends over, they all went to the hallway to puff. My mother wouldn't allow them to smoke in the apartment.

One winter, my father had pneumonia. He was really sick, and I was afraid he was going to die. He still went to the hallway to smoke—in his bathrobe, no less. I had no idea smoking was bad, nor did I have any idea smoking when you have a lung disease was even worse.

Smoking was just cool. The grownups did it, and it was banned for children. That made it doubly cool.

James Bond smoked. Three packs of Chesterfields a day. We didn't have Chesterfields. We had Tallinn and Extra which were regarded as good smokes. And then we had Belomorkanal, which was the peasants' cigarette.

My dad smoked the Tallinn brand. Named after Estonia's capital. They were the highest of the highest. And they were really disgusting.

Tallinn was the first brand of cigarettes I smoked, too. That pedophile Devon who Simon introduced me to, he got us Tallinn cigarettes for free. And there we sat, in his den, smoking and feeling like grownups, like James Bond, ready to conquer the world because we were fucking grownups and could do as we pleased.

It was a common punishment by parents or grandparents that when their kids or grandkids got caught smoking, they took them to the shed, made them smoke a whole pack and then watch them puke their guts out, thus making sure they'd never want to experience that feeling again.

But puking my guts out after having smoked half a pack at Devon's basement didn't do the trick for me. I wanted to keep doing it. Maybe it's because I

47

didn't get caught and it wasn't my parents or grandparents who had forced me to smoke until I was sick. Maybe it was because it was a conscious choice.

***

After I had puked my guts out that one time, I kept smoking whenever I could. I kept enjoying cigarettes in secret, quietly, trying my best not to get caught.

I couldn't shake that feeling one felt when inhaling the smoke, letting it run around in your lungs, feeling its calmness and excitement at the same time, and then exhaling, only to take another puff.

I was more addicted to the feeling of calm, peace, relaxation; the pleasure of the smoke running around in your body. At least before the physical addiction of nicotine kicked in.

But it was also a way of escaping reality for me. When we went to Devon's place, Simon and I—before we found out he liked little boys—he always had cigarettes ready for us. Or he walked down the block to the nearest store and got them. And Simon was my friend, he was actually being my friend, not trying to impress his other buddies with whom he would have to assume the role of being a bully.

We would just sit there, away from any troubles the real life would bring us; we'd sit there, smoke cigarettes, talk or sit quietly, just enjoying an alternate reality where I could be happy.

Alternate realities were great.

20

I hail from a long line of manipulative people. My great grandmother manipulated her husband—my great grandfather. Whenever she wanted something, and my great grandfather didn't want to grant it to her, she burst in tears.

"I will kill myself. One day I will kill myself. I don't have the courage now, but I will work up the courage and kill myself."

My great grandfather tended to her back and forth, catering to her every whim. Every time she didn't like something or wanted something, she threatened to kill herself.

She did that to me, too. I was at her studio apartment, bored out of my mind.

"Read a book," she told me.

"There's nothing to read," I replied.

She opened the cupboard door and took out a book by Maxim Gorky. "Read this."

"I don't want to. I'd rather read the book that's up on the top of the cupboard." Why would I want to read Gorky? The book looked extremely boring to me.

"I can't reach the book on the top of the cupboard," she said. But I kept insisting. She burst into tears, crawled on her knees to the cupboard—as if to demonstrate to me that she couldn't reach it—and kept telling me, "I will kill myself. One day I will kill myself. One day I'll have the courage to kill myself."

"I'm sorry! I'm sorry!" I yelled. "I will read the other book. Just don't kill yourself."

The eighty-something-year-old woman had successfully manipulated a child into doing something the child absolutely didn't fucking want to do. Had I known better, I'd solved the situation differently. But I was five or six. The fuck did I know.

And I was right. Gorky was the most boring writer ever. At least to a five or six-year-old. I have never ever picked up a book by Maxim Gorky since.

***

The manipulative bitch gene seemed to skip a generation. My maternal grandmother didn't seem to be that way.

"My mother got everything she wanted from my father, because she always threatened to kill herself," grandma used to tell me. I thought she told me that to indicate she wasn't that way.

I don't know about her first marriage to my grandfather—my mother's father. But in her second marriage to the love of her life—the guy I called pop-pops because he was much more in the picture as my grandfather than my actual grandfather was—I didn't notice any of those manipulative traits.

Unfortunately, my mother had inherited the trait of being manipulative.

She didn't threaten to kill herself, oh no. She did it way better.

"I will go away," she told me when I was being difficult.

I didn't want to eat my cereal, "I will go away." I didn't want to clean up after myself, "I will go away." I didn't want to bring firewood or the peat briquettes up to the apartment from the basement, "I will go away."

Every child is programmed to love their parents. And when a parent constantly threatens the child with going away, the child will develop a fear of abandonment.

That fear of abandonment has followed me throughout my entire life. Every relationship I've ever had, I've had this ingrained fear of abandonment—maybe one day they will go away, leaving me alone again in the midst of the crazy, scary world where I really don't want to be alone.

One time I was playing in the back yard of our Gutter Street apartment, and

I saw my mom leaving. I was maybe six or seven years old.

"Where are you going?"

"I'm going away," she said, and kept walking.

She had had a fight with my dad—they often fought—and she had gotten mad and went to clear her mind.

Was it my fault, I asked myself. I didn't know. My mind was rushing like crazy. Maybe they fought about me. Maybe I was the product of their marriage they didn't want, who was useless, who shouldn't have been born at all.

But I doubted that, too. I decided for myself that it wasn't my fault they fought. I thought they both loved me, but maybe didn't really know how to show it.

On the other hand, the fact that my mom left the house and told me she was going away scarred me for life. I would never forget that feeling of abandonment, that feeling of being completely worthless and useless.

A neighbor lady was also in the back yard.

"My mother went somewhere," I told her.

"I'm sure she's coming back," she replied. I wasn't. I was so confused I didn't even cry.

21

Things were changing.

The Soviet Union had started to crumble from every corner. "Mr. Gorbachev, tear down this wall," the American president, Ronald Reagan, had exclaimed, standing on a podium in West Berlin, just by the Berlin Wall. And mister Gorbachev didn't have much of a choice. The wall had become moot, the wall had to come down.

The history of the twentieth century that had been taught to us in school was bullshit history. It was the "officially approved" version of history that everyone knew was bullshit, but it was taught anyway.

"Estonia voluntarily joined the Soviet Union." No, it did not.

"The Soviet Union is a democratic country, formed by the working people." No, it was not.

"The freedoms here are much greater than anywhere else in the world." Nope. Just fucking no.

The people in Estonia and elsewhere in the Soviet Union and in the satellite countries were rebelling. The time was ripe; the Soviet Union was, on its own, on the verge of collapse and the people in the countries that had, for decades, been oppressed by the communist power, had finally stood up and were fighting for their freedom.

These were confusing times.

At school, the official program continued. Everything was done by the book, the entire curriculum was what the communist party had prescribed.

And yet, we all knew this was bullshit. We all knew we had been taught bullshit that had nothing to do with reality.

We all had grandparents who had been there before the commies came. Mine were especially fierce. But they were careful, too, because they had no way of knowing whether the rebellion would actually succeed.

My mother's mother and her husband—pop-pops—taught me everything about what I didn't learn in school. How Estonia had been a free country, a democratic country before the Soviets came. How the country's flag had been the blue-black-white tricolor some people were already waving again. How Estonia never "joined" the Soviet Union, how it was occupied by an evil force.

They taught me everything I had to know about what the "rebels" were trying to change.

But at the same time, they swore me to secrecy. I was never to utter a word about it to anyone. Despite the changing times, the KGB was still everywhere. And if a kid happened to say something that's not agreeable to the system, that kid's parents and grandparents were the ones who'd be in trouble.

Anti-Soviet thinking could mean twenty-five years in prison plus five years in a labor camp. It loosened up later in the 1980s, but you could still go to prison.

Anti-Soviet action could mean death.

We kept our mouths shut when adults were around.

When they weren't, we let it go.

"I knew Estonia's flag was the blue-black-white tricolor in the third grade," one student exclaimed.

"I knew it in the first," another bragged.

I doubted any of us had known anything.

22

Around the time when the "troubles" had hit, my parents got visas for the both of them, and my brother and I to go to Germany. East Germany, that is, because the West was still wishful thinking.

The way it worked in the Soviet Union was, you had to get an exit visa—that allowed you to leave the Soviet Union, something that was extremely difficult to get—and an entry visa to the country you wanted to visit—all but impossible to attain.

I guess my dad used his connections in the party hierarchy to obtain both. After all, East Germany was still under the influence of the Soviet Union, although the wall was crumbling.

My parents had been abroad, in the Soviet satellite countries, before. Mostly not together because the Soviet authorities were very suspicious if you applied to leave the country—even for a little while—with your significant other. That could have meant you're about to defect, and the Soviet Union couldn't afford losing people.

My mom and dad and his father had even been to West Germany before. But me and my brother had stayed home, as did my grandmother, so the danger of them defecting wasn't too high.

So, for the Soviet authorities to allow an entire family to leave was all but unprecedented. And yet, they did. It was highly suspicious.

We took the train. We had our own cabin, four bunk "beds," although those beds were more like wooden benches, built two and two on the walls of the cabin. It took two days to reach Berlin. Forty-eight hours of continuous travel to do a thousand miles.

***

The Germans were already allowed to cross the border. East Berliners and West Berliners were allowed to go back and forth through the wall at their convenience, they just had to show their passports.

"Can we go through?" my dad asked the East German border guard at the crossing at the Brandenburg Gate.

"No, I'm sorry," the guard replied and shook his head. After all, we only had visas for East Germany. Soviet tourists weren't allowed to go see what's on the other side.

It was to be another decade until I got to see what was on the other side of the wall. Even though, by that time, the wall was long gone.

23

Even though East Germany was a Soviet satellite state, it was considerably better off than what we were used to in Estonia. They actually had bananas at the grocery store at all times, readily available! No queues for anything, you could buy bread, cheese, meats, everything—they were just there.

Up to this point, I had thought a meal was ground meat sauce and potatoes, day in and day out. In East Germany, there was fish, there was meat, there was ice cream, there was bread, there were fresh fruit—and not just apples, but oranges, clementines, bananas, lychees, pears, whatnot. All the shit I had never even imagined.

Not even known it existed.

And there was something else. There was a choice of clothing. And footwear. My parents bought everything. They bought all clothes and shoes they needed for themselves and for my brother and I. And they bought a kitchen sink.

Yes, a sink. A two-bowl sink that was impossible to find in Estonia, they bought it in East Germany. Neatly packed in a cardboard box.

It was hideously brown. I knew my mother hated the brown color. But they bought it anyway.

This was my first experience with a smuggling operation.

They filled the two bowls of the sink with all the clothes and the shoes they had purchased. It was a lot, but they managed. It was illegal to import fancy— or fancier than the shit that was available in the Soviet Union—things even from the satellite states, so one had to get creative.

When the Soviet border guards and customs raided the carriage we were in, they asked about the box. My dad mixed up his Russian, wanting to say it was a kitchen sink, but what he really said was it was a toilet bowl.

The customs officer—a mean-looking Soviet bureaucrat—was so astonished that she didn't want to take the package apart.

If my dad hadn't fucked up his Russian at that moment, we might have not made it back.

24

My dad had a friend, an old lesbian lady who lived alone. Being a homosexual man was banned in the Soviet Union. Being a homosexual woman wasn't mentioned in the law, but it was frowned upon.

So most gay people—men or women—kept quiet about their sexuality and were either completely alone, lived with their siblings or, if they had been caught being gay, they were doing twenty-five plus five in some prison camp somewhere in Siberia.

Twenty-five plus five meant twenty-five years in prison plus five years at a labor camp. It was one of the harshest punishments in the Soviet Union, and a go-to one at that.

This lady had advised us to go visit some old friends of hers. Baltic Germans whose father had owned a pharmacy in Tallinn before the Soviet occupation. They had left Estonia for Germany when the Soviets were on their way to occupy the country, leaving everything they owned behind.

The town they lived in in Germany was, at the time, called Karl-Marx-Stadt, or the City of Karl Marx. No mystery there, considering. The town's actual name was Chemnitz.

"Who are you?" they asked us in German.

"We're coming from Estonia," my dad replied in Estonian.

"Oh my god, from Estonia!" the ladies exclaimed back, also in Estonian. They were about sixty years old. They hadn't seen an Estonian or spoken the language for fifty years.

And yet, they spoke perfect Estonian. That was astonishing to me.

***

It was in Dresden. The city bombed to the oblivion by the Allies during World War Two. Rebuilt by the Russians after the war.

We were staying at a guest house of my parents' friends. I'd occasionally get a permission to go out all on my own, to explore, to see what's around.

Her name was Anette. She was a little older than me.

We'd meet up under this old oak tree at the town park. I spoke a few words in English and German, and a few more words in Russian. She only spoke German, but we could understand each other.

She was way too well developed for her age. Beautiful blond hair. Big blue eyes that never stopped wandering. Boobs that would fit her mother. I did wonder how big her mother's boobs would've been. I guess I was a boob man even before I became a man.

We only met twice. We enjoyed each other's company.

We kissed once. That was a shame. I liked kissing Anette.

25

When we returned from East Germany to the misery that my every-day life was, I learned Simon had broken his foot and was in the hospital. Even though things were changing, in some ways, we were still in the dark ages. Simon was in a children's hospital that didn't allow visitors.

I was in a hospital once, a few years later. The times had changed enough for the hospitals to allow visitors, even if the patients were children. I couldn't have imagined staying there the week I did—let alone the three weeks Simon was in the hospital—completely alone, never seeing a friendly face.

It was a cruel regime that didn't allow hospitalized children to see their loved ones. There was no reason to it—it wasn't like it had been the time of the plague. It was just a rule for the sake of it. To instill power over people. To show who was in charge and all-powerful and made rules that didn't make any sense. The communist party did what it could to make its subjects lives as miserable as possible.

Fear. That's what the communists wanted. For the people to be afraid every day, every minute. To fear what might come next if they don't abide.

The next day after we arrived in Tallinn, I walked over to Simon's place. I had bought a can of Sprite for him as a gift because I hadn't had it before I went to East Germany and Simon surely hadn't had one ever. There was no Sprite in the Soviet Union.

"Oh, Elliot, Simon is in the hospital," his grandmother told me when she came to the door.

"What happened?"

"He broke his foot. He's at the children's hospital and they don't allow visitors."

"When is he going to get out?"

"Perhaps in a week or so," Simon's grandmother told me.

I had sent a postcard from Dresden to Simon. And even though visitors weren't allowed, parents were able to send packages to the patients of the children's hospital.

"He was so happy when he got your postcard," the grandmother told me. That almost made me tear up. I was glad I had made my friend happy.

When Simon got out of the hospital, I walked over to his house again. I gave him the Sprite. He was grateful.

He told me stories about other children in the hospital. One had ripped his liver apart in a bike accident. That was a cool story.

26

Simon and I used to go to a nearby forest and make bonfires. We collected dry branches, placed them in a safe fireplace and lit the fire. Since we both smoked, we usually had matches to light the fire with.

We had to hide the matches when we went back home. At least I did, considering I faced the third degree. Simon probably didn't. His father and uncle didn't care much, and his grandmother was probably innocent enough to think Simon wouldn't go down the road his father and uncle had.

How wrong she was. But some people have the tendency to see the best in us.

And then again, maybe I faced the third degree because my parents cared about what I was doing when out and about. But what I did know, should that have been the case, Simon had an easier life.

We had sat by the bonfire for some time, and the time to go home was around the corner. Responsible people put out the fire in the forest when they leave, so we decided to pee on it.

We took 'em out and peed on the fire.

"Ha-ha, you have a hard-on," I said to Simon.

"I don't have a hard-on," he replied.

"Oh, you do, that's a hard-on."

"I don't have a hard-on. It's just this big."

That was the day I learned all dicks were not created equal.

Of course, I had seen other dicks before. My dad's, for example. Which was big.

But I had thought it was big because he was a grown man and I was just a boy.

Simon was a year older than me, like all my classmates were. There was still hope.

27

Simon had two little dogs. Those things were mean, evil little rat-like beasts who barked at everyone and bit anything they could. Once, one of those little fuckers snapped my arm apart so badly that it was bleeding from every tooth hole the beast—the tiny beast, but still a beast—managed to inflict.

My friend Michael, on the other hand, had the sweetest dog there was. He was a rough collie, a smaller type than they normally are—"He had some sort of a dog polio when he was small, that's why he's smaller," Michael explained—always glad to see people he trusted, and Michael's friends were among them. He was an intelligent dog, he understood that if Michael trusted someone, he could, too.

I had always wanted a dog, but my parents would never grant my wish. I wanted a rough collie, too, but not because Michael had one; I wanted one because of Lassie.

There was this ongoing TV show about a yellow rough collie named Lassie. She was immensely intelligent and helped her humans out when they got in trouble—in the show, of course. The fact that Michael had a similar dog only enforced my belief that this was the dog I wanted.

But my parents refused.

"There's so much work with the dog."

"You have to walk the dog even if it's raining or snowing."

"The dog hair will be everywhere."

"We don't have enough room for a dog."

And many, many more excuses. It was like with a bike—I never got one because my parents were the masters of making excuses.

But all excuses became irrelevant when my mother got her wish—to get the dog she had always wanted.

It was an Afghan hound. She had always wanted an Afghan hound and she got one. Despite all the excuses I didn't get the dog I always wanted. Grownups can be dictatorial that way.

So, there we were. My mother and my father. My brother and me. Occasionally my widowed great grandmother. And a puppy that would grow up to be a big-ass dog—far bigger and hairier than a rough collie.

All in that three hundred and sixty-six-square-foot apartment that didn't have enough room for a dog.

It really didn't. But that had become a non-issue.

My parents paid one thousand and five hundred rubles for that thing. Sure, it was around the end of the Soviet Union and inflation was going crazy, but it was still an unspeakable amount of money.

That animal was the dumbest living thing to have ever walked the earth. The lime trees aligning Gutter Street were more intelligent. The bees pop-pops kept were more intelligent. I was sure I had met amoebas that were in the possession of a bigger brain than this excuse for a dog.

Afghan hounds are notoriously untrainable. No matter how much you try to teach them, they will never learn. And my mother's dog was a prime example of that breed trait.

It peed and shat everywhere. It never learned to ask to go outside. It never learned to do all its business outside when it was taken there—it came back from the walk and fucking shat on the carpet.

It wasn't allowed to go to my parents' bedroom. They closed the doors of their bedroom to keep the animal out. But soon it learned—quite on its own, to everyone's surprise—how to open the door by jumping on the door handles—and the moment it got into the bedroom, it went on my parents' bed and peed on it.

I should really call it a "she." It was a she. Its name was Sadie. Sadie Starlight, to be exact—it was a pure-breed Afghan hound from a supposedly excellent pedigree.

But how could I anthropomorphize a brainless entity? To have a name and other attributes of a living, breathing creature, that creature needs to have a brain. And it didn't qualify.

I often wondered, if this moron was from a good pedigree, how dumb did the other Afghan hounds have to be.

28

And even though I never got the dog I wanted, because "there's so much work with the dog" and "you have to walk the dog even if it's raining or snowing," that's exactly what I ended up doing.

I was the oldest kid, so I was sent out to walk the dumb animal. I was the one who did the work. My mother just wanted to possess an Afghan hound, but not really take care of it.

I was miserable.

Afghan hounds also need a lot of combing, otherwise their hair will stick together and create massive lumps of hair that need to be cut off. My mom spent more time cutting off the lumps than actually combing the beast.

And I didn't want to have to do anything with it.

***

The one thing Afghan hounds are famous for is their desire to run. They're almost as fast as the greyhound, but didn't possess ninety-nine percent of the intelligence the greyhound had.

So, when the stupid beast got loose from its leash—and it was able to pull its leash out of my hand when it saw something that piqued its interest—it just went off. It just ran along the street, a mile one way, a mile the other. It was almost a lost cause to catch the fucker, because to catch it, you had to literally catch it—jump on it when it was near you and hold on to it for dear life.

"Bring a piece of bologna," my dad told my brother one time when he and I were trying to catch the beast. It was running away from us at warp speed, then turned around and ran back, but, at warp speed, you don't catch a fucking cheetah. Or a dog equivalent of it.

Dad was hoping the smell of the bologna would attract it back to us. Little did he know that the beast would run past us, grab the piece of bologna he was holding in his hand and keep on running.

Finally, after it had run two marathons, it started to get tired. Since it had no brain, it didn't know where to run, so it kept running along the street back and forth. And when it came back towards us when already slightly tired, I just jumped on it and hold on to my dear life.

That's how we caught it, leashed it and brought back to the house.

This became a weekly occurrence.

I fucking hated my life with that beast.

One time it was chewing on a bone. I passed the fucker and it saw me as a threat, as someone who'd try to take away its bone. It jumped up and bit me in my arm so deep I was bleeding for hours.

Did I say I fucking hated my life with that fucking beast?

29

My great grandfather died when I was 10 years old.

This was my first experience with death. I was old enough to understand that people lived for a limited number of years and then died. I wasn't sure what happened to them after that. My mom was spiritual, she taught me that the soul lives forever and has the chance to be reborn as someone else.

I wasn't so sure about it. I had heard about heaven and hell. I wasn't sure they existed, either.

When I was a kid, every night I went to bed, I prayed. "I will never die. I will never die." Not much of a prayer, I realized even back then. And even though I had nothing to look forward to the next day, I clung to dear life. Life, living was too precious, too beautiful. I still never want to die. But at least I'm not afraid of dying anymore.

***

The Russian neighbors of my great grandparents—the ones who fought all the time—called my parents.

"There's been an accident involving your grandfather," they said.

My parents took off. They took the same two yellow, disgusting, time-consuming buses to my great grandparents' place.

A few hours later, my dad called. There was no phone in my great grandparents' house, so everyone who wanted to make phone calls had to walk to the phone booth around the corner.

The phone booth was this funny little invention. It usually stood on street corners and you could just walk in, pick up the phone, dial and then talk to anyone whose number you had. It cost two kopeks for a few minutes, and then the phone beeped and you added another two-kopek coin. If you didn't, the phone cut you off.

The kopek was the cent in the Soviet currency system. The ruble was the dollar. Neither of them was worth shit. And yet, they were incredibly precious.

My dad called our apartment. We had a phone.

"Pops is dead," he told me.

I didn't cry. I didn't know to. But I realized that the last time I saw my great grandfather was actually the last time I saw him alive. I sighed.

They buried him at a cemetery not too far from where he lived. They had a family plot here—lots of their relatives whom I hadn't met were buried there.

I shed a tear at the funeral. Funerals were sad, I didn't like them. Who would.

My grandmother—the daughter of my great grandfather and the mother of my mother—didn't.

"You didn't cry at your dad's funeral," I later told her.

"Did someone talk about that?" she asked.

Seriously, I thought, that's your question? Is it really about appearances all the time? Who gives a fuck what other people think, say or do.

I guess she didn't love her father too much. And that's fine, too.

30

After my great grandfather had departed this world, my great grandmother came to live with us for some months. In our three-hundred-and-sixty-six-square-foot, one-bedroom apartment.

I had slept on the couch in the living room. Suddenly, I was sleeping on the floor, on a mattress. Sharing the living room with my great grandmother.

She kept her apartment, too. She would sometimes go back there, tend to the garden, do some chores, and then she would come back to our place.

One day, she walked to the bus station, tripped, and fell. She broke her arm at her wrist. The doctor fixed her up good. She wore a cast for some time.

She was sad most of the time. "Fifty years. Fifty years we were married," she used to say. She didn't cry much, but was just sad all the time. Mourning is a bitch, I thought.

"I was married to your great grandfather for fifty years. How will I go on?"

I didn't know the answer to that question.

Go on she did, though. She moved back to her studio apartment eventually. She lived there alone for years. We'd go visit her now and then. She stopped mourning at one point. She even started to laugh and live again.

But she still had to carry water from the well. She was in her eighties, and wasn't the strongest of people. She was getting old and frail.

One day, I bought a plastic bucket and took it to her.

"I'm going to carry your water now," I told her. She was adamantly opposed to it. She knew carrying water was hard work and she didn't think I was strong enough to do it. But I was. And the plastic bucket I had bought was lighter than the iron ones she and my great grandfather had used most of their lives.

I went to my great grandmother's place every week, sometimes many times. To help her around, to saw and chop firewood, and, most importantly, to carry the water.

I carried enough water each time I visited so that it would last until the next time I went over. I didn't mind the work.

After all, she'd raised me.

31

In the fall of 1989, the fight for freedom of Estonia—and its southern neighbors of Latvia and Lithuania—had intensified. The Soviets still tried to impose their rule on the three occupied countries, so in response, the people organized all sorts of public protests to fight the oppressors and to restore their countries' independence that had violently been taken from them forty years earlier.

One of the protests that was organized was a four-hundred-mile-long human chain from the Estonian capital Tallinn to the Lithuanian capital Vilnius. Over two million people took part in the chain, to show the unity of the people of the three countries in their fight.

That human chain was called the Baltic Way.

I spent the summer with my paternal grandparents in that brick-and-mortar village. My cousins and I, we did all the normal kids' stuff we always did when we spent time together—played war, fought, ate the plentiful gourmet dinners my grandmother cooked, worked in the garden, went fishing.

But come August 23 of that year—the anniversary of the Molotov-Ribbentrop Pact, the non-aggression pact between the Soviet Union and Nazi Germany that included secret protocols that divided Europe between these superpowers and had put Estonia in the Soviet zone of influence—my grandparents and aunts set to leave to join the Baltic Way.

"I want to come, too," I told them.

But grandpa was resolute.

"It's no place for children."

My aunt protested that statement. "If it's not for children, who is it for then? It's for their future."

But gramps was adamant. It was no place for children, and I wasn't taken with them.

Maybe that was a good thing. I would've been out-of-my-mind bored. But because of my grandpa's inflexibility, I lost the chance to witness history.

32

My paternal grandfather was very strict. He had lots of rules. He could hit with an iron fist. Everyone was afraid of him—even my grandmother. I thought maybe the only person who wasn't afraid of him was my mother—because she had the balls to stand up against him.

I had the habit of biting off my fingernails. I never needed to cut them because whenever they grew even a hundredth-of-an-inch, I would just bite them off.

One summer, my granddad told me that if I hadn't grown any fingernails by the time I'd leave, he'd give me a beating.

Holy shit, did I try. Every single day, every single moment, I did my very best to stop biting my fingernails, terribly afraid of the beating I'd get. But I just couldn't stop, so my only hope was, he'd forget to check my fingers the day he was due to drive me back to Tallinn.

I don't think he forgot. We all went to Tallinn—grandpa, grandma, me. I was home already when he saw me biting a fingernail again.

"Oh, damn. You were supposed to get a beating if you didn't stop biting your nails!" he told me.

I was just happy I was home and he didn't have any power over me anymore.

I never received the beating.

But, truth be told, he was one of the two men in my life to influence me most—the other being my maternal grandma's husband, pop-pops. And I think my paternal grandfather's character, his entire demeanor was genetically passed on to me, skipping my father.

I, too, grew up to be this rough and tough asshole he was, I just learned to be less rough and less tough during the course of my life because the times we lived in turned out to be different.

As a rebellious kid, I didn't like him very much at a time. Only later I realized I admired and adored him.

He helped form me into the man I am today. Even though he never let me dry steer his ultra-expensive Lada. Not to mention drive.

33

All my relatives were poor to a certain degree. They didn't have much. They were just happy to have a roof over their heads.

My dad's sister, Sharon, she, her husband and her two kids—my cousins— had some of the shittiest of conditions.

They lived in the same, small, rotten village my dad's parents did. They had their own apartment about a mile from my grandparents' place. A one-bedroom apartment on the first floor. And a communal shitter. In the hallway. That was colder than an industrial freezer in hell in the winter.

Sharon had married a Russian. Dmitri was a nice, kind man. But he didn't speak a word of Estonian and that was troublesome for me because my Russian was not very good.

We were learning it in school, but we really didn't want to. Our overall anti-Russian sentiment also applied to the language, even though the language had nothing to do with what the Russian—or the Soviet—regime had done to us.

Sharon's kids, thanks to their father, spoke perfect Russian. I envied them. I wished I spoke perfect Russian, too. I could've spoken to Dmitri that way. But we didn't understand each other very well. We both did our best, though.

One day, in the middle of the day, I farted.

"Ha-ha, Elliot farted," my cousin Lena said out loud.

Aunt Sharon came to the room. "You need to go take a dump," she said.

"But I don't have to."

"When you fart, you have to take a dump," she insisted. She gave me two sheets of toilet paper—they kept their own shit paper at the apartment so that the neighbors wouldn't steal it from the communal shitter—and told me to go take a dump.

I obeyed. But I didn't shit. I didn't have to. It was just a fucking fart.

Staying at their place was hard. When I actually had to take a dump, I got the two sheets of toilet paper, which accounted for nothing, and then wiped the rest off with newspaper clippings that were all over the communal shitter floor.

Many people didn't have toilet paper. They used newspaper clippings.

I probably still have the mirrored prints of the nineteen eighties' news around my asshole.

34

Aunt Sharon's son, my cousin John, was a good friend. Whenever I spent time at Sharon's house or in the village they lived at, John and I were like two peas in a pod. We did everything together.

He was a few years older than me, but he wasn't a bully like my other cousin Roderick was. He was nice and kind and he always took me as his equal. While Roderick wanted to torture me and Lena, John was the calm voice of reason whose strength was equal to Roderick's, even though he was younger, and he protected his sister and me from Roderick's attempts to bully us.

Roderick wasn't an asshole or anything. We all did play together. John showed us how to make machine guns out of wood, and so we did. We played war, all of us together. Lena didn't like war games much, but John, Roderick and I, well, we played them all day long. Lena sometimes reluctantly joined, too.

One time John took me with him to the communal shitter in his building. He took a dump and later told me about American knickers.

"American knickers have very thin strips," John said, while rolling the strips of his underpants on his hips together. Once he was done rolling them, he added, "These are American knickers."

I believed him. I didn't know what American knickers were. He had read magazines, I hadn't.

A few nights later, we had a brief falling out.

We slept in the same bed—because there was no space to accommodate either of us otherwise. Evidently, that night didn't go well.

"You farted in the middle of the night," John said in the morning. "I had to go open the window."

I had no recollection of farting in the middle of the night. I'm sorry, I was asleep, I thought. I also thought people who were deep asleep didn't fart. Or didn't know about it.

We made up afterwards.

***

John and I, we played war all the time. He made World-War-Two type automatic weapons out of wood, and we ran around the village he lived in, shooting at the imaginary enemy.

"We're the Germans," John said. "We'll kill all the Russians."

My mind boggled around that. At school, we were taught that the Russians were the good guys and the Germans the bad.

John wanted to be bad instead of good.

"But the Germans are the bad ones, right?"

"Sure, but they're way cooler," John said.

His own father was Russian. I didn't understand how bad people could be cooler.

But all the wooden weapons he made, they were modeled after the German World-War-Two era weapons.

***

One day we were out in the woods when I suddenly felt the need to take a dump. But there was no toilet paper. Not even a newspaper.

"Use a tree leaf," Lena suggested. "Go shit under some tree and wipe with a random leaf."

That was weird for me. But I thought, maybe she knew about using tree leaves because of her mother's adamant stance about using actual toilet paper. Maybe she was just nature smart.

I did exactly that. I felt very dirty even after going through a ton of tree leaves.

It was different for the nature kids they were. They probably used tree leaves all the time.

I was from the city. I was used to johns and actual toilet paper. Not that the Soviet toilet paper was much better than a tree leaf. But at least it came in a roll.

35

I continued to be miserable at school. The bullying went on, daily. I was beaten in school, before school, after school. In one period, two of particularly cruel dickheads tripped me and made me fall, head first, into a cast iron radiator.

There was blood everywhere.

The school nurse couldn't do anything. She called my parents.

I was taken to the emergency room. I got four stitches. My head hurt like a motherfucker.

My class teacher in the elementary was very sympathetic to my troubles.

"Take him like a natural disaster," she told the other kids.

What a lovely human being she was, I thought.

***

As I couldn't get along with the assholes who bullied me—and with the ones that just despised me, resented me, didn't care about me or were just indifferent—my parents took me out of the school for a year.

I was supposed to be home schooled. I'd only go to school after my former classmates had left the building. I was to study on my own and then meet my teachers after hours to do the tests and get some additional pointers.

This was the best school year of my life. I could do all the studying in my own time—and that usually meant either first thing in the morning or at some point during the course of the day when I felt like it.

I had all the time in the world to just enjoy my life and have fun. It just turned out that it's hard to have fun without people your age around you.

I still hung out with Simon and Michael. They went to school full time, so our time horsing around, doing stupid kids' stuff was limited. I made a few new friends around my neighborhood, only to discover they were assholes, too.

Occasionally the bullies caught me when I went to school to take a test and they hadn't yet left. These days, it wasn't much different from actually going to school every day.

The homeschooling experiment ended at the end of the school year. In September, I was back in class. Back to the same misery.

Fuck me, I hated school.

36

The TV played an important role in my life. What else would a lonely, friendless kid do, where would he run away from the reality? Books? Sure. But the TV painted a picture, an actual picture, not something imaginary, something you had to put together yourself as with books. The TV was a lazy kid's book.

We had this small, black and white TV that stood in the living room. My parents watched it in the evening and I didn't have much to say what to watch, but during the day, after school, it was my source of entertainment. I watched cartoons and other children's programs from the local and the Russian TV channels, even though I didn't really understand Russian and had no desire to do so.

When I was older, however, I started to explore the wonderful world of TV little more. I discovered that we also had Finnish TV channels—something the Soviet authorities had tried to make impossible but in a true Soviet fashion failed.

The Estonian capital, Tallinn, lay only fifty miles south of its Finnish friend, Helsinki. Fifty miles—that's nothing for the TV waves to transmit. So, the Soviets tried to solve the problem—it was a problem because Western content was banned in the Soviet Union and it was dangerous for the regime if people educated themselves in the ways of the West—by erecting three tall steel towers in Tallinn that were supposed to interfere with the Finnish TV waves.

The people called the three towers "The Three Sisters." I kid you not.

But fortunately for us, the sisters didn't do much else than litter the city skyline. Whoever was interested in Northern Estonia could easily catch the Finnish TV waves and educate themselves not only in Finnish programs, but also watch American TV shows and movies the Finns showed every night.

MacGyver was my special favorite. Knight Rider, too. How I dreamed of having the survival skills of Angus MacGyver and the magical car of Michael Knight. I'd show all those assholes at school whose life mission was to make mine miserable.

Later, my parents brought home a color TV. That was even more magical than the old small-screened black-and-white box. Everything was in color, in real color, as if you looked outside the window and saw the real world. And that TV had something most of my schoolmates' TVs didn't—also the Finnish TV channels were in color.

Most Soviet TVs came without a chip that was commonly known as the "Finnish block." Basically, the chip was added to the TV and that made it possible for the TV to show Finnish channels which were transmitted in a different system than the Soviet one.

But many of those color TVs that people had, even with the "Finnish block," could transmit the Finnish channels black-and-white only. Many of my classmates had such TVs, and I instantly felt superior to them—even though during periods when I was beaten up, that superiority vanished immediately.

"I have a color TV," Troy boasted. "Only the Finnish channels are black and white."

"But my TV shows even Finnish channels in color," I said, not very modestly.

"That's bullshit," Troy replied. "No one can see Finnish channels in color but the Finns."

Simon was right next to me.

"His TV really does show Finnish channels in color," he told Troy. I felt good that Simon was willing to back me up.

Troy was still suspicious but didn't say anything. And I realized I didn't really have to convince him; I can just go home and watch MacGyver—or even James Bond—in fucking color. In my own mind, I ruled.

***

The best thing about watching Finnish TV was, I inadvertently started to learn English. And Finnish, too. All the American movies and shows were broadcast in their original language—English—and subtitled in Finnish,

85

which was very similar to my native language, Estonian.

My young brain started to put the spoken words and the written ones together, picking them up as I watched along. By the time we started to learn English at school, I was already able to somewhat speak it, although I only had some vocabulary and I knew how to pronounce; what I needed was the grammar.

And that made English one of my favorite subjects—I was actually good at it. I was a lot better than my classmates and that again gave my ego somewhat a boost.

Later I discovered that I had a knack for foreign languages—but only the ones I really wanted to learn. By the time we were taught Finnish, I practically spoke the language and only scored As. But with Russian, German and French, I did the bare minimum. I had no interest in these languages and I figured I never needed to speak them.

English, however, was the global language. That's what they spoke in America—where I wanted to go live one day. I had to master it.

And Finnish—I had friends in Finland. I loved to communicate with them in their native tongue, even though they spoke English, too.

I just failed to realize that any language you knew was a huge benefit. My dad tried to tell me that, but did I listen?

37

Now and then, we even had a video cassette recorder. The first one my parents brought back from West Germany. It was a chunky machine, almost the width of the television set itself.

That opened a completely new world for me.

Simon and I would go to the local video rental store in the Old Town and rent all sorts of movies we could get our hands onto. The trouble was, all these movies were dubbed in Russian. They were pirated copies of Western—mainly American—movies, oftentimes re-recorded hundreds of times, which meant the quality of them was abysmal.

And did I mention, they were all dubbed in Russian? And, when I say dubbed, I mean voice-overed. The Russians didn't dub the movies like the Germans or the French where an entire cast of actors and actresses provided their voices in their native language to translate the movie for their populaces who were incapable of reading subtitles and didn't know there's this thing called the English language around, let alone speak it.

The Russians were incapable of reading subtitles, too. They didn't know about the existence of the English language, either. But they were so useless and lazy that they didn't gather an ensemble of actors and actresses, they had just one guy who would do voiceovers for every movie there was.

And we were the idiots who rented them. We had been learning Russian at school, but we were far from understanding shitty voiceover translations of videotapes that had been copied over and over hundreds of times.

But on occasion, you could hear the original dialogue underneath the shitty Russian voiceover, and much of the dialogues could also be inferred from the visual. So we kept renting and watching them, watching the American movies that hadn't yet been released for TV and were years away from being showed even on Finnish channels.

One day, though, the video cassette player was gone. My mother had sold it.

"Why did you sell the video player?" I asked her.

"Because I was sick of your dad watching porn on it all the time."

Evidently, there was a video rental somewhere I didn't know about.

38

In school, throughout the years, I was an average student. Not the best really in anything, and not the worst, either. I had an okay brain, but as my parents constantly told me, I was lazy as fuck. Well, they didn't really say "fuck," but they sure meant it.

But school was torture for me anyway, so I did the bare minimum in most subjects, just to get by, just not to fail, just to get over with it.

And I was constantly bored. Both at school and at home doing homework.

Some say that interesting people are never bored.

The others, however, point out that smart people are always bored because trivial things don't interest them, only challenges. Maybe I was smart, even though I didn't feel particularly wise. But trivial things—among them schoolwork—surely didn't interest me. Who needs to know how much is the square root of eighty-one or what exact date Napoleon Bonaparte kicked the bucket? Who gives a fuck? I wasn't going to use this knowledge later in life anyway, so why would I study it?

My parents and my teachers may have been right, though, about me being lazy and talented. The bare minimum I studied came very easy to me and I could have just as easily studied more, gotten better grades and made my parents proud of the smart, talented kid they thought I was.

But then the laziness kicked in again and, as many times before and many times to come, I submitted half-assed tests or perfunctory homework and did things that I actually enjoyed.

How was I supposed to make myself do things that I didn't enjoy over the things I did? I had no idea. All I knew was, I had to pass my grades.

That I did.

39

Sometimes, though, good things happened, too.

My parents had many friends. Some were individual friends, some family friends. One day, some family friends visited us. They had a daughter who was about my age. Our families were friends with each other.

Somehow, she and I ended up boyfriend and girlfriend. It was puppy love, but we were too young to understand it anyway. She had long dark hair and beautiful, deep brown eyes. I liked her and she seemed to like me. This was all very new to me.

One time, we were sitting in my parents' bedroom, talking about this or that. We were in our early teens. If that.

"I have this friend," she said. "We pledged to be blood sisters. We sat there and then we decided to start sowing. We pricked our fingers and then put the fingers together. And then we showed each other our thing."

"That's cool," I replied. I didn't know what to make of that story. "I want to kiss you."

"Well, kiss me then."

We kissed. It was the first sexual contact I had ever had. It was intimate, it was passionate, it was everything a teenage boy would have ever dreamed of.

We made love that evening. This wasn't fucking, this was pure love making. Our parents in the next room, absorbed in their own debates, their own problems, their own issues. They didn't know, and they didn't give a shit. Which was good enough for us.

She lives in New Zealand now. New Zealand is beautiful. So was she.

40

I was almost never able to fight back against my bullies. They came en masse, and even if they hadn't, even if they had come alone, they would've still outpowered me.

They were strong, and I was weak. I was the little fat kid.

There was this one time, though, when some of them attacked me in the school back yard after classes. One of them took his dick out and tried to shove it into my mouth.

"Suck, baby, suck," he said.

A blind rage took over. I had never felt fury like this. It was as if I had stepped out of my body and just plain looking at it and what it as doing.

I was throwing punches left and right. I was kneeing those assholes' balls. I was punching their stomachs and jaws. I got a few punches in. I heard moans of pain. But they kept coming at me, too.

I lost the battle. My right eye was black and swollen. My fists and knees hurt. They beat me to my stomach with their feet. Nothing felt right.

I was lucky I kept all my teeth.

Nothing was put in my mouth or elsewhere that day. I just received the beating of my life.

When I had collected myself, I wiped the blood into my shirt, did my best to get up and limped home.

I cried. Not from the pain, even though my everything was hurting. It was the shame; it was the humiliation that made me cry.

When I was a kid, I never got to say, "You should see the other guy." I WAS the other guy. It was not pretty.

***

Oral rape was a thing of the time, evidently. The bullies tried to do that to the people they wanted to torture and humiliate. And the sentiment was weird.

We had all been culturally programmed to despise gays. The word "gay" wasn't even a thing. We called them faggots because that was what the law called them. The criminal law addressed homosexual men as faggots and specified that people who have been convicted of faggotry deserved to serve years in prison.

We all hated faggots. What kind of a man fucks another man in the ass, we thought. What's wrong with them? They needed to go to prison. Because faggotry never happens in prison. Right?

I hated gym to begin with. They made us do sports. Sit-ups, squats, climbing the rope, running, playing basketball or the Russian version of dodgeball, whatnot. All that wasn't for me.

But before gym, we had to go to the locker room and change from our school uniforms into our sports outfits.

Often, a much older class had just finished their gym class. They showered, too, after their class, while us, the younger generation, didn't do exercise as strenuous as them, or it was our last class of the day, and we could just go home and wash up there.

One day, the older class had just finished showering when my class came into the locker room. There was this guy who everybody called Death because his face looked like the caricatural face of, well, Death. The Grim Reaper himself.

He came at me, holding his dick in his hand.

"Hey, suck it, suck it," he said. I really didn't want to do that. I didn't want to punch him, either, because he seemed about ten feet taller than me. But he kept insisting.

Everybody laughed—his classmates and mine. All of them were having a field day. But I refused and I resisted. I don't know how long I could've held on, but the gym teacher walked in the locker room and the crowds dispersed.

The funny thing was, the common perception at the time was, whether you suck another man's cock, or you have your cock sucked by another man, you're a faggot. Nobody wanted to be a faggot.

And yet, Death was willingly trying to be a faggot and nobody faulted him for that.

I guess when you're trying to torture a weaker kid, you can't be a faggot even if you're trying to put your dick into another man's mouth. You'd be a hero.

41

Most of my summers I spent at my maternal grandparents' summer cottage. And that means my grandmother and her husband—she had divorced my mother's father a long time ago and they weren't really at speaking terms. They were civil enough at family gatherings, but that was the extent of their relationship.

"Why did you divorce your first husband?" I asked my grandmother once.

"Because I found pop-pops," she replied. I called her husband pop-pops because he was, most of the time, like my real grandfather.

I couldn't understand that. How can you just "find" someone else when you're married and have a child?

I found out later that it was completely possible and also, depending on the circumstances, healthy.

Pop-pops was the second man in my life to influence the most. Actually, in many ways, he was the first. My dad's father gave me his character, personality and demeanor; my mother's stepfather gave me life skills, he taught me to work and to love work. I can paint a house, grow tomatoes, keep bees and fix a coffee grinder thanks to him. And many other things.

I liked the idea of keeping bees. I thought I'd become a beekeeper in my own right someday.

But at the time, I was mostly afraid of him. He had an iron fist, too. And he didn't take refusal very well. At times, I felt like a slave on a plantation when I had to do all the chores he made me do. It took me a while to realize that I know how to do almost everything around an abode thanks to him.

42

I heard barking from the outside. Not the annoying type of barking you get from those little, nasty dogs that constantly bark. It was the barking of a big, proper dog, who usually stay silent and only bark when they have something important to say.

I wanted to see the dog, so I ran to the window and jumped on a chair to see better. But my planning wasn't ideal, and I hit my leg—right in the middle of it—against the wooden frame of the chair.

The pain was intolerable. I tried not to cry, but the effort was moot.

A big bruise developed on my leg. And then it kept growing. It was swollen, like an ugly deformity on my leg, all blue, and it hurt like hell.

After a few days, I decided to see a doctor about it.

She was a middle-aged surgeon with a very mild bedside manner. Doctor Guerra inspected the bump from every angle and then made up her mind.

"We need to cut that open," she said.

Fuck. That prospect didn't sit too well with me.

"We'll admit you to the hospital and we'll probably do the surgery in two or three days."

That prospect sat with me even worse. I didn't want to go to the hospital.

But I didn't get much of a say there. It had to be done.

I spent two very lonely days at the hospital before they took me to the operating room. My mom came to visit every day, a couple of my friends, too, but the visiting hours were only from five to seven in the afternoon and the rest of the time I was alone.

Well, alone meant I had a roommate, but he was an old man, and we didn't have much to talk about.

"On Monday, they're going to cut my leg off," he said.

"Why?"

"I got gangrene. They have to cut it off."

I felt sorry for him. I had seen people without a leg before, walking on crutches. When I was a kid, I saw one and asked him where his leg was.

"Oh, my leg is in my pocket," he said. At least he had good humor about it.

My mother told me then that his leg had been cut off because of a disease or injury, and it was not nice to ask cripples about their disabilities.

I never asked anyone about their disabilities again.

At night, the old man waiting for the amputation was in horrible pain. He kept turning in his bed, wincing and crying quietly, and then pressing the call button for the nurse to come and give him some morphine.

I didn't sleep much. His horrid pain troubled me. I wished his pain would stop. Once they cut off his leg, maybe it will, I thought.

The day of my operation arrived. I was taken to the operating room and given a local anesthetic. They didn't put you under for minor surgeries. My mother had told me a horror story about how she had had her appendix removed with a local anesthetic.

"The local anesthetic numbs your skin. When they cut you, you don't feel it. But you feel every bit when they mess around your abdomen, seeking your appendix and then removing it. I screamed the whole operation, that's how painful it was," she told me.

I thanked my stars I didn't need my appendix removed.

Doctor Guerra came in and was in her usual good spirits.

"Okay, let's do this," she said, after the anesthesiologist had done her bit. She scrubbed the massive, bruised bump on my leg with some disinfecting agent, took a scalpel and cut it open.

I was looking at the entire process.

"Do you want to lie down so that you don't see it?" the doctor asked.

"Fuck no," I said. "I want to see it all." Blood had never been an issue for me, although I knew of people who would faint at the sight of a drop of it.

The good doctor squeezed the bruise hard, and the clotted blood popped out of the cut. They placed a little bowl underneath my leg and the blood flowed around my leg into the bowl.

"Feeling all right?" Doctor Guerra asked.

I nodded. It was interesting to see what she was doing. It was fascinating to see my own skin cut open and dark blue blood and its clots being pushed out of the wound.

"Okay then, we're all done. Close it up," the doctor said, looked at me, smiled, and off she was.

The nurses sewed me up nicely and wrapped my leg into a thick layer of bandages.

The next day, Doctor Guerra came back and they opened the bandages.

"Okay. All's well here. Wrap it up again and send him home tomorrow," she told the nurses.

That they did.

"Scars make a man handsome," one of them told me and smiled. She was kind of pretty herself.

43

There was no religion in the Soviet Union—it was all but banned. There were churches, but nobody went there. The ones that did—they were under constant surveillance by the KGB and other repressive organs who kept a keen eye on the people and their activities. Religion had no place in a communist dictatorship.

A legend circulated among the more enlightened, the well-read folks that when, during the Second World War, Moscow—the capital of Russia and the Soviet Union—was under siege by the Nazi forces, then the Soviet dictator at the time, Joseph Stalin, ordered the Russian Orthodox priests to be brought back from the Gulag where he himself had sent them, to fly around Moscow and spray holy water at the city and its limits, in the hopes it would keep the Nazis out.

I had no idea if it helped or not, but the Nazis never entered Moscow. I had no idea if Stalin himself believed it helped the city, but people have the strange fascination with religion, and they turn to it when the shit has properly hit the fan, it's already all around you and there's no way of putting it back into the horse.

Stalin, of course—at least according to the said legend—immediately after Moscow was safe again, sent these priests back to the Gulag. They had served their purpose, and religion didn't have a place in a communist system.

Estonia was a Lutheran country. It had once been ruled by the Germans— and by the Swedes, the Danes, the Russians—and when Martin Luther's reformation came along, the initially-introduced Catholicism came to an end. Lutheranism was there to stay.

The churches were there. The religious sentiment was there. Just no one went to the church.

There were no synagogues—they were destroyed by the Nazis and never rebuilt because, you don't build new houses of worship in a place where religion doesn't exist.

There were no mosques because none of us knew what Muslims were or what Islam was.

But there were a few Lutheran churches around that just hung in there, doing nothing.

My mother's mother seemed to be religious, though. At least to a certain extent. She used to thank god, she used expressions like "god forbid," and she tried to instill some of it on me.

I wasn't a taker.

"How do you know there's a god?" I asked her.

"I don't. I just believe there is."

"But no one has ever seen god. How can you believe in something no one has ever seen?"

"That's why we go to space. That's why Yuri Gagarin went to space, and all the others who did. They're looking for god in heaven."

My mind was boggled. How can a grownup say idiotic shit like this with a straight face? I was eight years old and I realized it was idiotic. I was sure even Yuri Gagarin didn't believe he went to space to look for god. Did Neil Armstrong look for god when he was walking on the Moon? I highly doubted it.

But, sure. I let her believe what she wanted to believe.

Her husband, my pop-pops, was a much more down to earth person. He tended to the land, kept bees, and taught me how to be a farmer—even though I had no idea I should be one.

44

At times, I hated being at my grandmother and pop-pops' summer cottage—because I was made to work and work more than I would've preferred. There were times I would run to the forest behind the cottage, cursing, "Fucking old man, that fucking old man," meaning pop-pops. But eventually I would return from there, work some more, earn back my keep, and get to play some more.

It was beautiful over there. The cottage—a two-story log cabin with an attached log sauna—stood at a large plot of land, right by the forest that wasn't technically ours to use, but no one cared. Lots of our firewood came from the forest, and my grandparents had utilized some land in there for a fireplace, a compost pile and other purposes. It was the state's land, so why would anyone give a shit about that.

The plot had four cherry trees, one pear tree, ten apple trees, berry bushes and beds for strawberries and flowers, and a greenhouse for growing tomatoes and grapes.

Indeed, they tried to grow grapes in the Nordic climate. In a greenhouse, they might have even succeeded, but a muskrat had once chewed off many of the grape trees' roots and, after that, all we got were these teeny-tiny berries that weren't bigger than blackcurrant berries.

The grapes tasted very sweet. All the berries did.

Pop-pops heated the sauna every weekend and sometimes he invited the neighbors over. They would sit in the heat room, getting the temperature with humidity up to two hundred degrees and just sweat there, and then take a cold shower only to return to the heat room. It was called the Finnish sauna, although it was as Finnish as it was Estonian.

One time I accidentally went too close to the furnace and burned my hand.

"FUCK!" I screamed, uncontrollably, knowing that saying words like that in the presence of grownups would get me in trouble.

"Words like this you can only say when you have hair growing on your crotch," one of the neighbors told me.

I didn't have any hair growing on my crotch. I didn't say words like that in their presence anymore.

After sauna, the men got beers, opened them and drank them straight from the bottle.

People without hair on their crotch would sometimes get a sugary soda. Sometimes they wouldn't.

45

The next-door neighbor at my grandparents' summer cottage, Arthur, was a rich man. He was an old communist party figure who was so high up the party ladder that his work vehicle was a black Volga. The Volga was one of the most expensive cars the Soviet Union produced, and it was nearly impossible for a commoner to just go out and buy it—even if they had the money.

But the higher-uppers in the communist party sometimes got the chance to get one as their work vehicle. And very often, nobody kept taps on how these vehicles were used. That's how Arthur got away with driving the black Volga to his summer cottage.

He had a private vehicle, too. A Lada, the same kind as my paternal grandfather. To have access to two vehicles was almost unheard of. Somehow, Arthur had done very well for himself.

At midsummer eve—June 23—Estonians gather around a bonfire, and so did we, every year, at the summer cottage. The fireplace was in the forest behind the plot and it was almost always infested with millions of mosquitoes who feasted on our bodies. The bonfire only attracted more—and the smoke from the fire that was supposed to repel them was completely useless.

Another thing Estonians did on midsummer eve was grill meat. Chunks of pork were marinated in vinegar overnight and then, in the evening, when the bonfire had been lit, the pork was stuck on grilling rods and barbecued over hotter-than-hell charcoal.

The legend was that eating too much charcoal-grilled foods would cause cancer.

"Huh, now we're all getting cancer," Arthur joked one midsummer eve while stuffing his face with that golden, juicy, fatty barbecued pork.

"Sure we are," pop-pops seconded to him.

They both, sure as shit, got cancer.

Some things you don't joke about, I guess.

***

Pop-pops was diagnosed with stomach cancer in the summer of 1990. My grandmother and him were in and out of the doctors' offices all the time. He went to the hospital and had surgery—which my mother characterized as, "they opened him up and closed back up because there was nothing they could do."

He would sit in front of the TV, in his bathrobe. Occasionally he would wipe his eyes. He knew he was dying, and he didn't want to.

But nobody had even told him what he had.

In the Soviet Union, the doctors didn't have to tell the patients what they had. It was enough if their spouses knew. Who gives a fuck about the actual patient, right?

"If it's cancer, it's just one shot," he told my grandmother. He didn't want to live with cancer and die in awful pain. He wanted to get euthanized, even though that wasn't legal.

"It's not. Relax," my grandmother told him. She just blatantly lied to the love of her life.

And yet, somehow he knew.

His pain, at times, was intolerable. I didn't know what euthanasia was at the time, but if I had, I would've recommended it. Then again, to whom? His wife claimed he didn't have cancer, that he wasn't dying. I will never understand that.

One morning in March of 1991, the phone rang. My grandmother was on the line.

"How's pop-pops?" I asked.

"We don't got pop-pops anymore," she replied.

I sighed. "When?"

"Around two o'clock in the morning."

"Did he say anything?"

"He said, be friends," my grandmother said, but that was about her and his estranged daughter who had long hated my grandmother for having stolen her father from her mother.

They actually took his dying advice.

46

I had never experienced sorrow as such. He had really been my grandmother's love of her life. She cried all the time. She had loved her husband with everything she had, and now he was gone, and she didn't know how to go on.

I was twelve years old. I didn't know how to handle it. Fuck, I didn't know how to handle the death of a role model, let alone his constantly crying wife.

I tried to stay quiet. The entirety of it had overwhelmed me.

She sure cried at her husband's funeral.

I did, too.

He looked peaceful in the coffin. As if nothing had happened. As if he was still him. He was thinner than he had been when full of life, but quite similar to what he looked like when he was in his death bed. But he looked peaceful. Finally, his horrible disease was over, and he had found peace.

He looked as if he were just asleep. I guess he was. Just eternally.

He was buried in his home village in southern Estonia. Next to his father and mother.

My grandmother was buried there, too. Almost twenty years later.

47

Estonia was free. The Soviet Union was no more. It had collapsed faster than it had been born, and it was good that it was gone.

The politicians—some good, some horrid—started to rebuild the country.

They did an okay job. Many of them did a really bad job and demised into the trashcans of history. Nobody gave a single fuck about them.

***

The years preceding the independence and a few that followed were the hardest. The stores were empty. There was nothing to eat.

Once in a while, bread was brought to a store. A neighbor told another neighbor, "There's bread in the store, go get it!" The neighbor would spread the word. And the kids were sent to stand in the lines.

Oftentimes, when you were almost at the finish line, the storekeeper yelled, "That's it, we're out."

Well, fuck me blue. Why did I just stand in the line for two hours, in the deepest hopes of scoring a loaf of bread, or some bologna, or maybe some buckwheat?

An interim prime minister introduced coupons for things that were hard to get. Every family got a booklet of coupons that entitled them to a certain amount of bread, flour, potatoes, meat. Even gas.

If any of those couponed items were actually available, people could buy them according to how many coupons for a certain product they had.

People exchanged the coupons, even though that was illegal. Someone might have too many coupons for pork, while someone might have too many coupons for gas—or maybe didn't even own a car. They could trade to their benefit.

But everyone was still hungry.

It helped if you knew someone at the store—then you could get your hands on the really good stuff. That stuff was kept under the counter until. My grandma got a lot of under-the-counter foods. My parents—not so much.

For the kids, though, apart from having to stand in long lines to buy food, their lives went on as usual.

48

In April 1991, on my twelfth birthday, my mother's dad—my grandfather—came up with an idea.

"I want to teach you how to drive," he said. That was something I couldn't have even imagined. Long had I tried to dry steer every vehicle I had ever seen, but to drive an actual automobile, a moving automobile, damn, that was a dream come true.

One day he picked me up in his hideous green Zaporozhets—that was regarded as the worst car the Soviet Union had ever produced—and we took off to his summer cottage, a little ways out of town.

The Zaporozhets was the Soviet Union's answer to Porsche—in the sense that its engine was in the back. In every other aspect, it was the anti-Porsche. Or it was meant to imitate the original Hitler-mobile, the Volkswagen Beetle. And even though the Beetle was regarded as one of the worst cars in the world, somehow the Soviets managed to make the Zaporozhets even worse.

Its engine had air cooling, which didn't work most of the time, so it was a common sight in the summer, seeing Zaporozhets drivers at the roadside with their deck lids open, trying to cool the engine. When the temperature hit the eighties, the air wasn't cold enough anymore to cool the engine, so their only option was, when the engine had overheated, to pull over and let it rest for a while.

A hundred-mile journey in a car like this could take five hours, with all the cooling breaks. I guess the poor Soviet man was supposed to have a ton of time in his hands. And the reality was, they didn't.

The Zaporozhets was built to accommodate five people. Only two would fit semi-comfortably. Maybe one person on the back seat would be equally semi-comfortable, but they'd need to be very tiny.

It was just my grandpa and me, driving to his summer cottage. He pulled over once we had exited the city.

"Okay. You need to be very calm about this," he said. I nodded and waited for further instructions.

"You need to give just a little throttle and let go of the clutch really, and I mean REALLY slowly. Otherwise, the driveshaft is going to break."

Okay. Really slowly. "Remember, very slowly. If you break the driveshaft, I can probably fix it before we have to go back, but then, the driving for you will be over."

I didn't want my driving to be over before it had ever started. So, there I was, sitting in the driver's seat. I turned the engine on, put the transmission in gear and did everything like grandpa had taught me.

And I shit you not, I was moving! We were moving! The tiny little hideously green Zaporozhets was fucking moving!

***

I didn't break the driveshaft. I managed to let go of the clutch as slowly as grandpa had taught me. I was driving on the highway at forty miles an hour—because the Zaporozhets didn't go any faster—and I felt like the king of the known universe.

I drove about twenty miles to his summer cottage. He gave me pointers all along the way. The Zaporozhets didn't have any side mirrors, so the only way to look back was the rear-view mirror, and if you needed to change lanes, you needed to look over your shoulder.

Fortunately, that wasn't necessary. At forty miles an hour, I never needed to pass anyone. And there were no lanes to change as there weren't any. Just one lane south and one lane north. We were going south.

At the cottage, we did some gardening. And grandpa fried some potatoes for lunch.

"I always boil the potatoes before taking them here, then frying them is a lot easier."

It sure was easy. We had lunch in no time. Fried boiled potatoes. There was nothing else, but we were thankful for each bite. We had food.

***

He was the only adult in my life who let me use swear words. He treated me as a human being, as a grownup. And he had taught me one of the most valuable skills in life. How to drive stick. In the worst car the humankind had ever produced.

Thanks to him, in later life, I could drive anything. I could drive a fucking washing machine to the fucking Moon.

49

My dad worked at a government ministry at the time and one of his chores was to take care of some elderly people who weren't able to take care of themselves anymore. He found the perfect elderly.

The system was still the same. You couldn't buy a new apartment and sell your old one. Or, well, you could, but you had to have shitload of money to buy one and you couldn't sell the apartment that was in a house that might be returned to its rightful owners.

Since the house we lived in on Gutter Street had been nationalized when the Soviet occupation began, there was a real chance it would be returned to the heirs of that person. Of course, that was the right thing to do, but it would also make a lot of people potentially homeless.

It was the time of great opportunity.

The people my dad was taking care of were an old couple, living in a one-bedroom apartment right in the center of Tallinn. We, too, were living in a one-bedroom apartment, but twice as small as the one he had his eyes on. It would've been a massive upgrade.

The way he did it was, our family and that old couple exchanged apartments. They were supposed to live in our small apartment while we got to live in theirs.

Only the old couple wanted to go to a nursing home. Or maybe it was their kids who wanted their parents to go to the nursing home. In any case, my dad managed to officially exchange the apartments. The six-hundred-and-thirty-five-foot one-bedroom apartment was ours and the three-hunded-and-sixty-six-foot one-bedroom apartment was someone else's. Definitely not the people's we exchanged apartments with, and definitely not anyone's after the house was returned to its rightful owners.

Quite out of the blue, I lived in the very center of the city. And I suddenly had to take the streetcar to school.

The building itself was an ode to the Stalinist architecture. It was built in 1951, when Joseph Stalin was holding the entire Soviet Union in an iron grip, killing anyone who disagreed with him and sending millions of people to the Gulag prison camps.

In the Soviet Union, there were many distinct schools of architecture. There were the Nikita Khrushchev-era apartment buildings with very small rooms and very low ceilings—because you had to sparingly use the space. There were the Leonid Brezhnev-era dormitory buildings, built from concrete blocks that wouldn't withstand a perfect storm.

And then there were the Stalinist buildings. Built from brick, they normally had massive rooms, high ceilings and they were all five stories tall. There was a law in the Soviet Union that all buildings with six or more stories needed to have an elevator. Five-story buildings were a huge money saver.

Our apartment on the third floor of that hideous, green-colored building with about a hundred apartments also had lavish rooms. You walked in, you faced a long hallway that connected all the rooms. The first one on the right was the living room. The second one on the right was the bedroom.

Then, at the end of the long hallway, you found the john. Right next to it, the bathroom. Bear in mind, this was an actual Soviet ideal—a separate room for the shitter and the room you bathe in. I could see the appeal.

And then, at the right of the bathroom, it was the kitchen. That's where people would cook and eat. It was almost the law that you don't eat anywhere else than the kitchen. That's where the dining table was; where else would you eat.

At least I made some new friends there.

50

The ninth grade was a particularly hard year for me. The bullying had wound down over the years, but I really, really didn't want to go to school. Everything was different, everyone's expectations were higher—we had to apply to different high schools and had to show good grades—and schoolwork was boring as fuck.

Who wants to learn things like math and physics and chemistry—shit they'd never use in real life anyway.

I skipped school most of the first trimester. I went out with the few friends I had. We drank, smoke, fucked around. We did everything we weren't supposed to do.

***

There was Corey. He lived in the same building I did. His setup was close to Simon's—he lived with his father and his grandma, sans the uncle Simon had.

There was Roscoe. He lived with his mother and father in the next building over. They had a big dog who only responded to Finnish because they had lived in Finland for a while and gotten the dog while they were there. Roscoe also had a little brother he seemed to love very much. They were a very harmonic family—something I had no experience in.

There was Clark. He was the most like me; nobody really liked him, and he seemed like a bullied soul who needed a friend. Later, he turned out to be an asshole like the many other people I would come to encounter in my travels.

And then there was Gary. He was this adopted kid of my neighbors who hated everyone, especially people living in the same building. They actually denied us access to our storage box in the basement to the extent that they changed the key to the main basement door and gave the new key to everyone in the building but us.

When I had gotten the key from a neighbor and copied it, and tried to access the basement, they "accidentally" showed up and tried to take key away from me.

"You don't know how things work in this building," they told me. Wait, what? I can't access my own basement storage box because things don't work like that in this building? How about you go fuck yourselves, eh, I thought.

I never went to be basement again. It was too complicated. But I did fuck up Gary's dad a few days later. He was a special kind of asshole.

51

One day, I was smoking in the hallway, on the balcony, with the doors open. It was perfectly legal these days, and no one knew any different.

And Gary's dad, quite suddenly, came out of his apartment and saw me smoking.

"What the fuck are you doing here?" he asked.

"I'm enjoying my cigarette," I replied.

"Whose cigarette butt is that?" He pointed to a lone butt on the stairs that I sure as shit didn't throw there. I threw my butts out of the balcony.

"I don't know."

"It's yours. Pick it up!"

His wife, Gary's adoptive mother, also came out of the apartment and joined the yelling.

"It's your butt, pick it up and throw it away," she screamed.

I thought the entire scene was quite hilarious.

"How about you crawl back under the rock you came from," I suggested. I had no intention of picking up someone else's cigarette butt from the stairs. What the fuck does it have to do with me anyway, I thought.

Gary's parents kept on yelling, and I yelled at them, trying to defend myself.

Then Gary's dad went back to the apartment, and when he returned, he was carrying an iron bar. He was holding it up as if he was going to hit me with it.

"For the last time, pick up the cigarette butt!" he yelled at me, waving the iron bar.

I didn't have much of a choice there.

I carried a can of mace for protection. And I needed protection right there and then.

I probably sprayed half of that can at Gary's dad. He whined. He was all but blind. But he lowered his iron bar, and Gary's mother was so shocked at what had happened that she just walked herself and her husband back to their apartment.

I had won a battle against mean grownups. I was proud.

***

A couple of days later, I was asked to go to the principal's office in school. I didn't think I had done anything wrong, so I went, happily. The principal was an asshole, but he was also reasonable—if you really didn't do anything, he wouldn't fuck with you.

There were two police officers.

"What did you do?" the principal asked.

I had no idea. "What did I do?"

"Well, we have this complaint from your neighbor that you maced him and he's blind from one eye now," one of the cops told me.

Holy fuck, I thought. I actually blinded the motherfucker? Well, serves him right, I thought. But, am I on the hook? How do I get off it?

"I'm sorry that he's blind from one eye," I said, "but he came at me with an iron bar. I had to defend myself."

"So, tell us the whole story," the other officer said.

I did. Maybe I wasn't very convincing. But I did know I was in the right and Gary's parents—and the cops—were in the wrong.

"Fair enough," the officers said after I had told the story. And I thought that was the end of it.

***

A few days later, I got an invite to the local police station. I met with the commissioner of the station and the two officers who had come to my school.

"You're a crook!" the commissioner told me.

"I'm sorry?"

"You maced an innocent man. You're a crook. You're going down."

I shrugged and repeated my side of the story. "If that motherfucker is an innocent man, then I'm Mahatma Gandhi," I told him. "He came at me with a fucking iron bar. I just defended myself."

He shook his head. "You're a crook. You can go to jail for this."

I shrugged. "I don't give a fuck," I said. "I did nothing wrong. I defended myself."

I stood up and left the room.

The cops never bothered me again about this. I guess I was, indeed, right.

Gary's parents hated me till the day they croaked. Good riddance when that finally happened.

With Gary himself, I got along fine. Until we didn't. Turned out he was a fag.

52

We didn't know much about how the world worked, me and the people we interacted with. We, the children of the Soviet Union, only knew what had been taught to us by our parents, our teachers, our friends.

And we knew that faggotry was a criminal offense. We didn't know any better. The word "faggotry" was actually written into the law.

"You know Gary's a fag, right?" Clark asked me when we were playing computer games at his place.

"How do you know?"

"I suspected it. So I rented a fag porn movie and made him watch it. He started to jerk off."

"Wait, what? He started to jerk off in your apartment while you were watching?" By that time, I had learned that you only jerked off when you were all alone in an extremely private setting.

"Well, I left the room and watched in hiding. He got aroused by the fag porn and took his dick out and started to jerk off," Clark said.

"But why would you watch?" I couldn't comprehend. Maybe Clark was a closeted fag, too?

"I wanted to prove that he's a fag. He's definitely a fag."

My relationship with Gary declined after that. I didn't want to be associated with a fag. They fuck other men in the ass, I thought. Or get fucked by other men in their asses. The idea was horrendous.

It took years of growing up for me to become tolerant, accepting of everyone. Back then, I was just an ignorant little asshole. We all were.

53

Finland was just fifty miles north of Estonia, over the Gulf of Finland, by ferry. It was the country every Estonian yearned to go to because it was in the West; it was the closest Western country to the Estonian people who were trapped in the Soviet occupation.

Some Estonians had been there. Some had relatives there who were either ethnic Finns, or ethnic Estonians who had escaped the Soviet occupation, taking a huge risk during the Second World War and sailed a refugee boat there.

Some of them, who didn't get bombed during their journeys by either the Russian or the German air forces, and made it to safer shores, stayed there, in Finland. Some moved on to Sweden, Germany, the United Kingdom, or even the United States.

Michael's parents had friends and relatives in Finland, and he had been there many times.

Mostly, the Soviet authorities didn't allow whole families leave to the Western countries all together—they feared that if an entire family leaves, there would be a good chance none of them would come back, they'd ask for asylum and be granted one.

But Michael's parents were also essential workers in the Soviet Union, so the authorities' presumption was, they would return. After all, their family had always been well taken care of.

"Everywhere we went, we had the KGB follow us," Michael told me. The KGB was the most repressive of the Soviet internal repressive organs—the committee of internal security.

It had almost unlimited power domestically; abroad, it spied after Western governments and the few citizens of the Soviet Union who had been allowed to visit Western countries.

"Even before our trip, we'd hear clicks in our phone calls, as if some stranger who had hacked our phone line was listening in, picking up the call and hanging up. We had strange phone calls coming into the house."

The KGB was everywhere.

My parents had been to Finland, too. Without me and my brother, because leaving us behind would ensure their return. A communist dictatorship can't function without people; every person who escaped to the West was a massive loss for the dictatorship.

But soon after the Soviet Union collapsed, my parents' friends in Finland suggested I should visit them.

They had two daughters, one a year or so older than me, and the other one the age of my brother. We were sort of friends, even though we had met each other only a few times they had come to Estonia. Finns liked coming to Estonia because they could buy cheap booze. Some came every weekend.

So, there I was, holding a Soviet passport even though the Soviet Union had ceased to exist. A Finnish visa in the passport, because you needed to apply for one and you were lucky to get it. Embarking on a ferry journey to Helsinki all by myself.

My parents' friend Regina came to meet me at the harbor and then she drove me to her home in the small town of Kotka, some eighty miles east of Helsinki.

The ferry journey took four hours. It was a very slow ferry.

And the process of getting through the border control of customs took another two. Everyone who disembarked the ferry was questioned, their passports were triple checked, their visas were read with a magnifying glass. The Soviet Union had ceased to exist, but the people coming from what used to be it to the West were still screened under a microscope.

We were unreliable people, and no one wanted us in the West.

A part of me understood it, too.

54

Regina was awfully nice. She treated me as a distinguished guest, she gave me an entire room at her house to feel at home—which, coincidentally, was her younger daughter's room, who had been deported to stay with her sister—and she catered and cooked and took me and her daughters places I didn't even imagine existed.

Like an ice cream stand. An ice cream stand that had tens of different flavors of ice cream. Just pick and choose. What the fuck is "nougat"? Back home, you had one type of vanilla ice cream with chocolate coating and that cost more than any kid had in their pocket. In Finland, that was something anyone could just go and buy.

Regina's daughters were equally lovely. Patricia, the one a year older than me, took me on bike rides in the neighborhood, and she hung around when we went on trips with Regina. Daisy, the one my brother's age, hung around too.

I got into an argument with Daisy. She liked to hang around me, and since I was staying in her room, it was her right.

"I actually need some privacy," I told her once.

"This is my room," she said.

"But I want to change my clothes."

"So change them."

I wasn't comfortable with taking my pants off when a girl was present. In a sexual setting it would have been different. But this was anything but.

"Can you please fuck off so I can change?" I asked her, very politely.

She finally relented.

"But this is my room," she still emphasized.

I understood that. I just didn't want to swing my dick at her.

***

The way they—Regina, Patricia and Daisy lived, was different from the way me, my brother and my parents lived. So different that I couldn't even understand it.

They kept a stash of cash in their living room cupboard.

"Mom, can I take some cash?" Patricia asked her mother, whisperingly, as if trying to hide it from me, before we went out.

"Of course!" Regina replied. Patricia went to the cupboard and got a fifty-mark bill. In Finland, that was probably not a big chunk of money.

In Estonia, that was around two hundred crowns. Some people—especially the retired people—got that much in a month.

We had never had a cabinet that had money in it. I had never even had any pocket money. And yet, just fifty miles north of us, there was a country where kids could just walk to a cabinet and take out a bill of money worth the same as some people's monthly wage in a country I came from, and spend it according to what they wanted to spend it on.

The Finns are related to Estonians, ethnically. But their customs were very different from pretty much anyone.

"Mom, let's make some coffee," Patricia said one night. It was eight o'clock in the evening. In Estonia, people only drank coffee in the morning. The children didn't drink coffee at all. It was forbidden to them by their parents. Well, some kids with more liberal parents did, but still, only in the morning. Drinking coffee at night, that was something out of this world.

One night, Patricia and I were watching the TV. We were sitting on a couch and MacGyver was on.

Suddenly, Patricia farted. It wasn't a big one. My mind raced as to what had happened.

When I farted, I would get a big telling of and a lecture from my parents. Farting, where I came from, wasn't something you did in the presence of anyone else. It was like jerking off.

Well, according to the Soviet Estonian folklore, jerking off was something one wasn't supposed to do at all. Farting was kind of allowed when you were alone in a forest where no one could hear—or smell—you.

And there was this girl, farting just like that, without any remorse, without any shame, as if it were something completely normal.

The fact was, it was normal. For the Finns, at least. In my later life, I interviewed a Finn for a job. She farted during the job interview.

"Oops, a small fart," she said. Any other employer in Estonia would have sent her off in shame. But I had learned that farting in Finnish culture was a norm. It was what people did, openly, publicly, without shame. It was normal.

Good for the Finns. Surely everyone enjoys a good fart now and then. And letting it go without any false shame—good for them. Everyone should have less false shame.

We're human fucking beings. We release bodily functions. I thought, how was that a taboo?

55

My mother had sold the video cassette recorder a few years earlier because she resented my dad watching porn. Well, then he found another source of it—porn magazines.

There were none back when Estonia was still occupied by the Soviet Union. But when the country restored its independence, porn magazines were some of the first publications that appeared on the shelves of the newsstands.

Boy, did he love to buy and read those. There were two different magazines that were both published every month. He made sure to buy both of them.

It didn't take any hard work to find the stash. I started to read them, too. And I actually did read them. The pictures were nice, sure, but the stories, the highly erotic—and many hardcore pornographic—stories were on par with the pictures of the models.

One of the magazines published "Josephine Mutzenbacher or The Story of a Viennese Whore, as Told by Herself"—a famous pornographic novel by an anonymous author or authors, first published in Vienna, Austria, in 1906. That novel, published in pieces every month, was the most eye-opening sexual textbook I had ever read. I was immersed in it, I read every paragraph, every sentence, every word. It was well written, but it also talked about a world that was so alien, but yet so desirable for a young boy who wanted to fuck every woman in the world, but just didn't know how to commence the mission.

I didn't only jerk off to most of the pictures of the naked women in the magazines. The stories they published were equally jerk-offable. I'm glad my dad just kept the stash and only read the new magazines he bought; the old ones had to be disgusting by the time I had gotten through with them.

One evening, the fucking bitch of the dog had broken into the living room. It was running amok like the crazy beast it was.

Dad stormed in, to help me get the beast out of the living room. He had a massive hard-on. It was all I could see. Seeing your father's hard-on cannot be good for your health, I thought.

"Get out, get out of here!" he screamed at the beast. The beast did fuck off. Maybe it was scared of my dad's boner.

I brushed it off, though. He was probably reading a new edition of one of the two porn magazines and rubbing one off. No harm there. I just wished he hadn't burst into the room like that. Sometimes the greater good isn't saving your living room from a moronic canine; sometimes it's saving your face in front of your son.

One day, the stash was gone. I couldn't find it anywhere.

"Where the hell are all the porn magazines?" I asked him.

"I threw them away," he said.

You threw them away? "Why would you do that?" I asked.

"I don't need them anymore."

But would it have killed you to stop and think that maybe I did?

I told Clark about it the next day.

"Well, hide his car keys," Clark said.

"The fuck good would that do?" I asked.

"Tell him you throw them away," Clark suggested. "He threw away something that were yours, so you throw away something that's his."

The logic was faulty, but it was there. With one caveat.

"But these weren't my magazines. They were his."

Clark shrugged. He didn't have any more solutions to offer.

56

The one thing I hadn't taken in account about moving to the city center was… Russians. Up to that point, I had been rather spared from the Russian bullies because they didn't live around the small Gutter Street apartment. But in the city center, things were different.

There were quite a few Russian gangs in the courtyard of my building and some others around it. They all hated each other, but there was another entity they hated a lot more.

Estonians. They loathed the Estonians. As badly as we loathed the Russians.

So my new favorite pastime became running away from different Russian gangs. As if my regular bullies weren't enough, I needed to deal with a new nemesis.

One of the gangs was particularly vicious. When they caught a group of Estonians in their hands, they wouldn't just beat us up. They would torture us.

The most powerful gang had a leader by the name of Andrey. Everyone called him Okha. Okha meant a little off the grid—or, well, a complete retard. He lived up to his name.

One time when they caught me, they put me in a steel tub at a construction site we had sneaked into to have some privacy to smoke.

They set the steel tub rolling down a hill. I tried to grab the edge of the tube to stop it. It ran over my right-hand fingers and broke two of them. I can't imagine physical pain worse than feeling your bones break.

Those motherfuckers. I hated them with all I had.

**

Okha's gang had a girl in it. She was as beautiful as the ocean sunrise. Or the ocean sunset, I can't tell the difference.

Larissa was about my age; she was the sister of one of Okha's gang members. She had been around the courtyard for months, and we had exchanged a few words in the past, but nothing serious had ensued.

She had light red hair and was freckled all over her face, but her face was kind. She didn't belong to the gang, she had just gotten in it to impress her brother—or, probably because her brother had made her. Larissa was incredibly nice.

I fell head over heels in love with her—just by seeing her around. I had butterflies in my stomach over her and I wanted to make her my wife and lifelong companion.

"I'm in love with Larissa," I told my friends. "She's so pretty, I can't stop thinking about her."

I don't know who, but one of them ratted me out to the Russians.

***

The next time I met Okha, he didn't beat me up, though. He didn't even break any of my fingers.

"So, you're in love with Larissa?" he asked me.

"What do you know about that?" I asked back.

"Eh, nothing much. Why do you like her?"

"None of your business, fuckhead."

Okha smiled at me. "She sure is beautiful."

I nodded.

From that day forward, Okha's gang never bothered me. That was fine with me.

I never got to make beautiful love to the beautiful Larissa, either. She moved away with her parents. And she didn't show any interest in me, either.

All I did was, get back in the apartment and rub one out, thinking of the beautiful Larissa who could've been my wife. My hand must've had blisters all over it.

But the Russians didn't fuck with me anymore. Maybe because I had taken affection to one of theirs.

I'm fairly sure if Larissa and I had become an item, they would've chopped me up and dropped the pieces in the sewer. I guess I was lucky.

57

The apartment we moved in to, in that hideous green building with neighbors meaner than rattlesnakes, that must have been cursed. Or maybe it was blessed. Maybe it had a wormhole to an alternate reality where people realized the truth of their relationships.

It was the apartment where my parents split up.

My mother had a lover a few years before. He was known as Uncle Preston. I have no idea how serious that was. My mother and father never spilt up over him.

But that time, my mother was serious. She had gotten involved with a transcendental meditation cult—the one that apparently the Beatles and some other famous morons were involved with—and it had succumbed her entirely. And she met Uncle Leland.

They moved in together, not far from where we lived. Uncle Leland was actually a pretty cool guy, even though, being in my teens now, I never had to call him Uncle. He was this old Chernobyl veteran, very calm, reasonable, and approachable guy that I didn't mind being my stepfather.

One day I walked over there, spent some time with them and then walked back to the apartment. I smoked a pack of cigarettes while walking back, but that had nothing to do with my visit.

I puked my guts out after that.

"It's because you went to your mother's and Leland's place," my dad said. "It stressed you out."

I agreed. But just for the appearances' sake.

***

"Do you love your mother?" my dad asked me.

"Like every kid," I replied.

"Do you love your father?"

"Like every kid."

He was crying. I did cry, too. My parents, however faulty they were, were splitting up. There was Uncle Leland who didn't belong. Even though he was nice, he didn't fucking belong. How was I supposed to accept this guy as a substitute for my dad?

58

I learned the hard way that marriages in the Soviet Union—or even after the Soviet occupation—weren't designed to last. There was an ongoing belief that over half of the marriages wed in the Soviet Union were bound to fail—and they were. A man always married the first woman who touched his dick. Or a woman always married the first man who touched her cunt.

Maybe any first marriage wasn't supposed to last. At least when we subscribe to that belief. But that was a fact in the society the Soviet Union had created.

I also learned the hard way that my mother and father weren't going to stay together. And that they had had lovers outside of their marriage all along the way.

My mother had Uncle Leland. Years ago, she had had Uncle Preston. She might have had others along the way, too.

My father, as it turned out, had had a lover in East Germany for decades. I had never met "Aunt Miranda" my dad had been fucking all the years he ever visited East Germany, but the realization that my parents had lovers outside of their marriage came as a shock for me.

He might have had others along the way, too.

"Your father has had lovers all along our marriage," mother told me. "This is not a unique situation."

I guess I was too sheltered from all the drama, only being exposed to bits of it.

It turned out I wasn't that sheltered as it all actually happened.

I promised myself I wouldn't do that to myself. I would always be faithful to my life partner.

Then again, I promised a lot of other things to myself. Promises to oneself don't really matter.

At the time, though, I strongly believed in my ability to keep my promises.

***

Some people aren't just supposed to be together. My mother and my father, they were never supposed to be together. It wasn't meant to be for them.

I'm sure they loved each other, at least once upon a time. Or maybe they thought they loved each other. Or maybe they just lacked options. It was like that in the Soviet Union. Sometimes you just fucked and married—or married and fucked—the first person of the opposite sex that came along, had a bunch of kids and were miserable for the rest of your life.

I didn't have a problem with divorce. I had a problem with getting together when the people were clearly incompatible.

My father was a down-to-earth bureaucrat, an employee of the state, who went to the office every day, did what he was told to do, came home in the evening, had a beer, and went to sleep.

My mother was an esoteric, she was always looking for spiritual causes that would—at least in her own mind—better herself. She got hooked on transcendental meditation—that bullshit that the Beatles, or at least John Lennon, used to do—and when that world opened to her, she also found Uncle Leland that was became the last straw in her marriage.

She and Uncle Leland didn't stay together. They stayed friends after the brief stint my mother lived with him, but at the end of the day, my mom decided it was better for her to live alone.

And that was okay, too. We all needed to find what makes us happy.

59

My dad seemingly got over my mother. While she was dwelling with Uncle Leland, my dad, working for the government, met Hanna. She was from Berlin, Germany. Her family was engaged with all sorts of social work and they had recently discovered Estonia. Hanna and her mother traveled to Estonia frequently and my father fell in love with Hanna.

Apparently, Hanna also fell in love with my father. They got married in a beautiful ceremony.

My mother and my father had gotten divorced one day before their twentieth wedding anniversary.

***

Hanna was really nice. And her family was rich, and she was quite well off herself, too. She and her mother used to take me and my brother Danny on shopping sprees. We got new jeans, new sneakers, new T-shirts, new jackets, whatever they deemed we needed.

We ourselves didn't know what we needed. They did. We got all sorts of fancy clothes.

The problem was, they didn't realize that much of the stuff sold at stores in the early nineties in Estonia was counterfeit. I got new Puma sneakers, only to realize that they were actually named Plima.

Another reason to get beaten up at school. How refreshing, I thought.

Hanna often gave me and Danny pocket money, too. More than we could imagine. When I got twenty Deutschmarks pocket money, I felt like I could buy anything. I could buy a horse if I wanted to, I figured.

I settled for booze and cigarettes. What would I have done with a horse?

60

What one wore was an issue of one's status. If one wore brand clothes, really nice ones, one would be king or queen. If one wore shitty clothes—especially counterfeit ones—one was liable to get bullied or worse.

During the Soviet occupation, everyone at school had to wear a uniform. I detested that uniform. It made us look like the military, but that was the regime's point.

When Estonia restored its independence, we suddenly got to wear whatever we wanted to school. No one gave a shit anymore.

The kids from the richer families wore fancy clothes. Levi's jeans, Tommy Hilfiger T-shirts. Whatnot. They either had families out West, or their families were doing well enough to buy these clothes from the black market. No one was able to buy any of those clothes from the open market because in the open market, you thought you were buying Puma sneakers and you got Plima ones instead.

I was one of the kids from a poorer family. I had fake Wrangler jeans, sown up by some Russian sweatshop employee in a basement in Leningrad. I was wearing the Plima sneakers Hanna had bought, although in good heart, but they were still fake Pumas.

"Did she really think these were authentic Pumas?" Simon asked me.

I shrugged. "How the fuck was I supposed to know?"

"You read the fucking label," he said. He was right. I hadn't paid any attention.

But in fact, the clothes Hanna had bought were the first nice clothes I had. I didn't mind them being fake. They resembled the originals. They were great.

They weren't great in the eyes of my school mates. I was still the underdog, only then, I was also wearing shitty, fake clothes that only a poor person would wear.

But there were poorer kids around. Some of them wore clothes sown by their parents. They had it much worse than me. They were treated as if they weren't human beings.

I felt sorry for them.

It shouldn't be a shame to be poor. But in that setting, there was nothing worse.

61

At first, when Hanna and my dad got together, he continued to live in Estonia and she stayed in Berlin. He would go over there for some time and then Hanna would come over to Estonia for some time.

During the divorce, my dad, who years earlier quit smoking, had started again. He used to be a pack-a-day smoker, and the split had put such a stress on him that he started again.

I didn't blame him.

But whenever he went to Germany, he quit. Hanna's mother didn't like smoking, so he flew to Germany, stopped smoking for some weeks and when he came back and I met him at the airport, I handed him a pack of cigarettes.

We smoked together outside of the airport after he had collected his luggage. My parents had gotten used to the idea that I, too, smoked. There wasn't much they could do about it, really.

Until one time, when I again was meeting my dad at the airport, I gave him the traditional pack of cigarettes and he rejected it.

"Thank you, son, but I don't smoke."

What the actual fuck, I thought.

"You always come back from Germany and start again," I said.

"Not this time. I quit."

That he actually did. He quit for good. He never had another cigarette again.

I quit many times, too. It was the easiest thing in the world, quitting smoking. Like Samuel Clemens, I did it many times.

62

After my dad permanently moved to Germany, one summer he and Hanna invited me to visit. But flying was outrageously expensive—when my dad flew, he made them out to be business trips, so his employer paid for them—and I had to take a bus.

The bus left Tallinn at seven o'clock in the morning to embark on its thousand-mile journey—literally, the distance it drove was a thousand miles—from Tallinn to Berlin. It went through Latvia, Lithuania and Poland, stopping at each of these countries' capitals where people could stretch their legs, get something to eat or drink, or get off or on the bus if they had reached their final destinations or were starting their journey.

I sat next to a blond, blue-eyed girl who was probably about five years older than me. She went to Germany to university. She took the trip many times a year because she was from Estonia, but studied in Germany, so she now and then wanted to go home, but needed to go back to school, too.

We got to talking and she helped me pass the hours. The journey took twenty-three hours, so there was a lot of time to kill, and a lot of boredom to fend off. The bus showed movies from teeny-tiny TV screens, but they were all voiceovered in Russian, so only the Russian passengers took interest in them; the rest of us passengers were indifferent and tried to keep their minds busy with other things.

We played cards, we played battleship; whatever to keep our minds occupied and not to succumb to the lonely abyss of boredom.

In the evening, when most people had already gotten tired of watching Russian-language movies and were setting to fall asleep in their seats, she suddenly put her hand on my crotch.

"Do you want to have fun?"

Sure, I was down to having some fun.

She slowly opened my fly and took it out.

"You wanna?" she asked, smiling at me. She wasn't particularly pretty and I certainly wouldn't have fallen in love with her, but the thrill of doing something naughty on a bus, full of other people who could potentially see it, overcame any objection I might have had.

Not that I had many. Teenage boys always walk around with a hard-on, even though, most of the time, they have nothing really to do with it.

She gave me a marvelous blowjob. She even swallowed. Then she smiled at me, turned around and went to sleep.

So did I.

When the bus arrived in Berlin in the morning, she gave me a kiss on the cheek and went on her way.

Turned out taking a twenty-three-hour bus ride wasn't too bad.

63

The Berlin Wall was long gone, although bits and pieces of it still remained, scattered around the city. Berlin, due to its history, became my favorite city in the world. No other city encompassed so much history, so many events, so much tragedy and such interesting sites. Checkpoint Charlie, the Tempelhof Airport, the Reichstag building, Alexanderplatz—it was just overwhelming and fascinating at the same time.

When my parents, my brother and I had visited Germany by train in the nineteen-eighties, we only got to see East Berlin. My dad and Hanna, however, lived in what used to be West Berlin, right in the middle of what was the American occupation sector. Not far from Hanna's house was the Clay Headquarters, the main American military base when the United States was occupying a part of Berlin. The downtown of the American sector wasn't far, either. Nothing was really too far. I could take a train anywhere in Berlin and arrive there within an hour.

Hanna had two sons who were roughly my and my brother's age. Her oldest son, Rudolf, and her youngest, Hannes, became my stepbrothers. We were all good friends, too. I had finally encountered kids about my age who treated me so well that I couldn't believe it was actually happening.

Germany didn't have any taboos about smoking and drinking. Both were legal when you were fourteen and, shit, that's what me and Rudolf did a lot. He introduced me to many of his friends—and many of them hated my guts. I was this loud-mouthed Eastern European who cursed all the time, didn't speak much German—we conversed in English—and I was only there because Rudolf's mom had probably made him take me.

But I didn't mind. We smoked cigarettes—Gauloises, the French brand, that became my favorite smoke—and we drank gallons of beer. We didn't have a worry in the world. And German beer was just so fucking delicious. The swill they called beer in Estonia, its smell and taste felt like ancient history. Even though I knew perfectly well I had to go back there.

Maybe I was a loud-mouthed Eastern European who cursed all the time to Rudolf as well. But he never showed it. He only showed me step-brotherly love and even if it was his mother who made him take me places and show me around, he never complained. He always accepted me as I was. He was just a genuinely good person.

His brother, even though we didn't interact that much, was quite the same.

And my father, who had always been this nervous wreck while he was married to my mother, who would yell at me or have serious words when he felt I did something wrong—he was a completely different person. Calm, nice, easy to be around with, supportive, talkative. Something had so changed in him.

I thought he was just happy. For the first time in his life, he was actually happy. Good for him.

64

The one thing that I came to learn about the Germans when visiting my father was that Germans had no shame. During every visit I made, at least once it happened that I woke up in the morning, put my clothes on and went to the bathroom to get rid of all the liquid I had consumed the night before, and Hanna would be walking out of the bathroom, completely naked.

"Oops, sorry," she said and walked back to her bedroom.

I would never walk around naked, anywhere where strangers were in the house. And yet, for Germans, it came naturally.

A German parenting book said to teach one's children that mommy and daddy bathe together and that was completely normal.

Maybe it was. In Germany. It wasn't for me. As much as I liked Hanna as a person, to walk out of your bedroom early in the morning, still sleepy, and then see the naked, wrinkled body of a fifty-year-old woman... Not something a teenage boy would like to see. It was like jumping in cold water—you could feel your dick shorten a few inches and your balls jump back into your stomach.

Later I would also learn that the Germans particularly liked anal sex. Between a man and a woman. Not that this was troubling information, but it seemed to be a very German thing. Fuck if I know why. Maybe it's the history. Maybe the Germans always wanted to be the Roman Empire because all sorts of sexual deviance were a norm for the Roman Empire.

Wanting to be the Roman Empire, though, had led Germany into a lot of trouble at times.

65

My mother had a friend who was a movie producer at the local, state-sponsored movie production company. And she agreed to take me on to her new project—a joint venture with a huge German movie conglomerate that wanted to take advantage of the newly-independent Estonia with its low wages, but scenery that actually fit the movie's plot.

It was a film about Germans living in Russia, near the River Volga, during the Soviet times. It was a tragic plot, about human relations, about the hatred and discrimination of Germans in Russia, about Shakespearean love, about betrayal. Being part of a movie crew was something I had never ever done and I found it immensely fascinating. I could work, earn my own money, and learn about history.

I liked history. The real one, not the one I had been taught in school for so many years.

It wasn't easy for a thirteen-year-old boy to be part of the crew, an all-adult crew where most of the people were old-school prudes who, according to the ingrained rules, firmly believed that children were an annoyance.

But I met some really cool people, too.

Interestingly, the Germans treated me much better than some of the Estonian members of the crew. I developed a particular friendship with this German actor. He treated me as an equal. He never looked down on me. He was a kind man. He was my favorite of the entire crew.

He went on to be famous, and not only in the German cinema, but worldwide. I never met him again after our cooperation with that film crew ended, but I always knew he was my friend.

He died of cancer years later. That made me sad.

The German director and assistant director also treated me great. They didn't think I was their equal, but they treated me as an essential worker to their project, and that was fine with me.

I was a fourteen-year-old boy, thrown into a grown-up world, everything was new to me, but I felt fine. I felt superior, at least to my peers back home.

***

I was making my own money, too. I was actually working for money, I was earning a living. I was making so much money that I could buy a car. If only I had been old enough to drive one.

I was making a thousand crowns a week. For comparison, an average Estonian retiree made two hundred crowns a month, and they made do. They had to.

The crown was the money in the newly independent Estonia. It was modeled after the Scandinavian crowns, but was worth a lot less. One Deutschmark was worth about eight Estonian crowns. But then again, the cost of living was so much lower in Estonia that the comparison isn't valid. A pack of semi-shitty cigarettes cost eight crowns in Estonia and three Deutschmarks in Germany.

You catch my drift.

I missed the first month of my high-school tenure because of that. But I had a lot more fun during those months working with the film crew than I had had during my entire high school. It was fucking worth it.

***

They stopped shooting for a while in the fall but planned to continue in the winter. I wasn't sure if I were to be invited back to join the crew. But the Germans insisted I come back, even though some of the Estonian old prudes didn't want me there.

"He can only come back if he promises not to swear," an old prude said at the meeting where they decided who would come back and who wouldn't.

I promised not to swear.

I continued to swear. Fuck that old prude bitch, I figured.

66

The movie hired a few horses from a local farm. Even though it was set in the twentieth century, in the 1950s and the 1960s' Soviet Union, you needed horses for farming since normal, motorized farming equipment wasn't available or was horrendously expensive. So, people used horses.

The two horses were tended by two girls. Carla and Peyton. Carla was blond, quite good-looking, but didn't do anything for me.

Peyton, however, was the dream. She was a tall girl with beautiful long black hair, with blue-ish eyes, and when she looked at you, you felt shivers all along your body. When she smiled, you wished she'd smile at you. When she frowned, you wished she'd frowned at anyone else than you—and that you could be there for her, hug her, caress her, take away the reason she was frowning. She looked like perfection, like a ship that had been built in a bottle, but better.

The endless nights I spent thinking about her. Jerking off like crazy, not minding the blisters.

There was a legend that if you jerk off too much, your palms will start growing hair. I found out the hard way that it was just a legend.

As much as I tried to hit on her, she never responded. It was like hitting your head on a barn wall, repeatedly, trying to garner her attention but never being successful.

She was a young boy's dream and a nightmare, bundled together into one beautiful entity.

***

One of the location managers at the movie set, a middle-aged Jewish guy called Benji became a friend of mine. And when I say middle-aged, I mean in his thirties. I was fourteen, for fuck's sake. Everyone older than me was middle-aged.

We talked about many things with Benji. Our pasts, our potential futures.

"My dream is to go to Israel," Benji told me. "I'd go there, live there as a Jew. It's not like life is bad here, but it's better there."

"My dream is to go to America," I said. "I've always wanted to go to America."

"Sure, go. If you get the chance, go," Benji said. "I just dream about Israel, every time I close my eyes, I dream about Israel. I've never been there."

Neither had I.

"I just want to go anywhere. Estonia isn't for me. I would just fuck off if I could," I said.

I also told him about my feelings for Peyton.

"So, your dream is to fuck Peyton from the behind and then leave the country?"

"Yeah. Why not."

Yes, that was my dream. To fuck Peyton to the oblivion, to fuck her to the point her eyeballs popped out, and then take her with me to my travels around the world, hopefully settling in America.

That was the dream.

Benji was one of the best people I had encountered.

67

I never got to fuck Peyton. It wasn't meant to be. She paid no attention to me. I had no other choice than to give up.

Lara was one of the stagehands. She was always around. She had this hands-on approach to everything. She needed to be everywhere at the same time. She was kind of a role model for the other stagehands.

She also was near me all the time.

I used to use the antenna of my walkie-talkie to stroke her delicate parts.

"Hey, dipshit, leave my ass alone!" Sorry, ma'am.

"Hey, dickhead," she said, "leave my pussy alone!" Sorry, ma'am.

She was sweet.

I could tell she would fuck me. And I could tell she'd actually teach me things.

She did. That night we spent together was very educational. I learned so many things. I learned how to lick pussy. I learned how to move, what to stroke, how to stroke, how to do my best to give a woman pleasure. I learned that, being a man, my job was to give pleasure.

I felt like the king of the world, even though I was just a student.

The next day Benji told me she was the crew slut. That she had slept with everyone and she would continue to do so.

I didn't give one single fuck. I had the lesson of the lifetime. And Lara was a brilliant teacher.

There also was something satisfying about having slept with an older woman.

It caressed my ego that a woman who had the option of sleeping with someone who could teach her something chose to sleep with someone who needed educating.

She must have seen something in me. She must have even somewhat liked me. And that made me feel good. Powerful. I was the king of the world.

68

Oftentimes, the shooting ended past everyone's bedtime. But then, the Germans would have already anticipated it and there would be cases of booze waiting for the crew.

Gin.

Vodka.

Tequila.

Whiskey. And whisky. Those two are different things. Whiskey is American and Irish. Whisky is Scottish.

Oh my god. Cases and cases of hard liquor. At two o'clock in the morning. Just to wake up at six o'clock and go to work again.

And I'd drink. I'd drink it pure; I'd drink it with a mixer.

I hated gin. It smelled bad, it tasted bad, I wouldn't want it to touch my lips.

"That's bad. I don't like it," I said.

"Hogarth Gin is bad, you think? Hogarth?" one guy asked me.

As if that were the issue. All gin was bad. I didn't like gin at all.

Juniper is a nice tree. Just don't make shitty booze out of it, I thought.

They meant well, though. We had lots of other boozes together.

This was the most liberating time in my young life. I was still a kid, but I was smoking like a chimney, drinking like a camel—and I did all that out in the open. There was no adult supervision—hell, it was the adults who brought the booze.

Nobody cared I smoked. Nobody cared I drank. Nobody cared I fornicated. Nobody would tell my parents. I was having the time of my life.

***

Most importantly, I was making money. My own money, money that was for me only and free for me to spend as I saw fit. And I was making astronomical amounts of it—at least in my own head.

While working with the film crew, I didn't even have to spend any of it. Free food, free hotels, free booze. Nothing to spend my money on other than things I wanted to spend it on. I knew I was set for the entire coming schoolyear and then some.

***

My parents always had a weird attitude about money. Even money that wasn't theirs but supposedly mine.

Years earlier, I had helped one of our neighbors with some gardening work. She had come into the possession of a one-dollar bill. That's one American dollar—a banknote most people in the Soviet Union hadn't even seen, let alone possessed. The neighbor was so grateful for my help that she gave the dollar bill to me.

Soon after, I took the dollar and went to a special store that was meant for foreigners only. They sold Western goods and for hard currency only. I bought Western chewing gum and candy.

When I returned home, my parents were curious as to where I went.

"I went to the currency store," I said.

"WHAT?"

"I had the dollar, I wanted to buy gum and candy."

This created a scandal that took the proportions of Watergate. I was yelled at, lectured about the value of money, and I didn't even understand what I had done wrong. After all, it had been my money, mine to spend.

"This dollar was worth thirty rubles!" my father screamed at me. "We could have bought two pounds of kielbasa with it!"

And there I was, crying, knowing that I had done a terrible thing because they, my parents, told me so, but without understanding why it was terrible. It was my money! Mine. I had earned it. And even though I liked kielbasa, why would I use my money to buy it? Wasn't it their job to provide food for the family and have me have the little fun I could with the money I myself earned, I asked myself.

This time, though, I knew things were going to be different. I worked my ass off for the big bucks I made, and I was going to spend it on things I wanted. Which mainly constituted smokes and booze, but they didn't need to know that.

And they didn't even want to control my spending by that time. Maybe they had figured out that my money was mine? Or maybe they realized that if I was capable of working and earning, then I was grown up enough to have control over what I used the money for?

Not that I cared, really.

69

When I finally made it to high school, the classes had already started. Since I had missed the first month, I was this awkward addition to my class where I knew almost no one.

In the elementary school, we had three classes at the same level—class A, class B, and class C. In high school, there were only two—class A, specialized in sciences, and class B, specialized in the arts. I was in class B, obviously, because I couldn't think of anything more painful than to be in a class that specializes in math, physics, and chemistry. I didn't like the arts either that much, but I figured that it would at least be easier to sail through it, get my diploma and fuck off into the real world.

In my class, I knew only a few people. About half of the class were kids who had been in in class B or class C in the elementary—I had been in class A— and about half of the kids were complete newcomers from other schools.

Moreover, there were six boys in my class. And almost thirty girls.

In a normal setting, this would have been paradise. This would have been a setting where the boys could fuck a different girl every week throughout the schoolyear. Well, almost. As I said, I wasn't very good at math.

In reality, however, every single girl—be it from the parallel classes or complete newcomers—already knew: I was that little fat kid, that little dipshit who was bullied for the first nine years of school and who was regarded as a worthless piece of shit. Just an annoyance. Just a "natural disaster," as one of my teachers had once put it.

Simon was the only boy from my previous class who had remained in the same class as I had. Michael left for another school closer to his home.

Steve was a kid who had joined the high school class B from the elementary class C. I had seen him around, but never really interacted with him. Mick was from the elementary class B. Didn't know him well, either.

Charles was a completely new addition. None of us knew him. James was another one, but he didn't last long. He wasn't one of the best and the brightest in any kind of a setting and he soon left to pursue avenues closer to his intellect.

70

Before starting high school, I had a bit of a growth spurt. I wasn't the little fat kid anymore; I was thinner and taller and looked pretty much normal.

Maybe the summer work with the film crew helped. Maybe it was just biology and growing up.

But the hardcore bullying had died down. Well, it had grown from physical torture to more of an intellectual one, at least at times.

We had all grown up to a certain extent, so I—and my schoolmates—had matured to the level where interjecting hurtful comments would be more of an asskicking than an actual, physical asskicking itself.

But intellectual violence was something I could deal with. With words, I could be as vicious as a brown recluse if need be. And I knew that carefully chosen words can hurt. After all, they had hurt me.

Charles was one of the most creative types of all of us boys. He was also a bit of a pervert. He wrote short stories that were disgusting as hell, but those stories provided us with amazingly great entertainment.

One of his stories, titled "Pizza," was about a guy who ate too much, puked his guts out and since the puke looked like pizza, he ate it again, from the ground, using his hands.

Another story was the Little Red Ridinghood, but the Little Red Ridinghood was actually his dick. James's ass was the Big Bad Wolf, and the Big Bad Wolf ate the poor Little Red Ridinghood. And then, according to the story, he'd pee into James's ass.

Despite of being a pervert, he had all the markings of becoming a great writer. His fantasy was, perhaps, a little off the course, maybe catered for a specific, not a very healthy audience, but the talent was definitely there.

Charles became a lawyer instead. That's a huge loss for the literary world.

But his stories sure were hilarious to our young minds.

71

Going to class every day, a class of only six boys and almost thirty girls did have its plus side, though. Every day, I got to look at all these girls, fantasize about them, fall in and out of love with them. I may have been in love with half of them at any given moment, but they wouldn't give me the time of day. In their eyes, I was still the loser I had been in the elementary.

Many of them were gorgeous. Some were less so. People are, first and foremost, superficial beings—we develop attraction based on the outer beauty before we get to see the inner one. We fall in love with the looks and start loving the person inside. Sometimes we don't start loving at all.

The most gorgeous girl in my class was Olivia. She was tall, she had natural red hair and had freckles all over her face that complimented her face. She had a beautiful figure—not athletic, but thin and feminine. When she talked, when she walked, grace was all over her. She had this ability to make the person she talked to the most important person in the room.

Everyone loved her.

I adored her.

She was 29B. That was her bra size.

How would I know? She told me. We would talk about anything.

I adored her and I was so deeply in the friendzone that I couldn't believe it. Or I could, but refused to.

I don't know why she and I became friends. Maybe she was intrigued by me, by what I used to be in the elementary and she wanted to find out for herself what kind of a person I was. And maybe she liked the person I really was, but only as a friend.

I loved and adored her, but she only liked me. That wasn't a bad thing. I got to be in her vicinity, and that, even though it made me shiver all over my body and the butterflies in my stomach got viciously angry, was a good thing.

She liked older boys. Most of the guys who circled around her were one or two years older than our class. And I was a year younger than everybody— including Olivia—in my class.

Olivia didn't believe she was the most beautiful girl in our class. Or she was just modest.

Her best friend, Laurel, had been Miss Estonia. Olivia was convinced Laurel was the most beautiful girl in the class. But all the guys knew otherwise. Laurel was all right; Olivia was a fucking goddess.

I invited her to a party once, a party at my parents' apartment while they were out of town.

"I'm in love with you," I told her. "I can't help it."

She looked almost sad.

"Please don't be," she said. She hugged me and kissed me on the cheek. "There are too many guys in love with me already." Ain't that the truth, I thought. Who wouldn't be in love with her?

She never stopped being my friend. Even after I confessed my undying love for her. She shot me down, but did it with such gracious ease that I could never hold it against her.

Maybe I just liked her too much to be angry at her. Besides, it was her choice whom to like or love or sleep with, I thought.

All I was left with was my love for her and my right hand.

72

There were other girls with whom I was in love in my class as well. They never became true friends of mine like Olivia had.

One actually left for another school because of my constant attempts to hit on her. At least that's what Charles told me. He may have been lying. I never got to ask her.

Another one ended up being Charles's prom date.

One I absolutely adored I didn't even approach. She looked inapproachable. She had short blond hair and thick lips and she was taller than me, and I was deeply in love with her, but she always kept the company of other girls. I never saw her talking to a guy.

I just looked at her from afar, thought about how she could be my girlfriend, but never had the guts to approach her.

I was sure she wouldn't want me, either, pretty much like all the other gorgeous girls in my class.

I had to look outside of my class to get girls, that much was clear.

But I could still enjoy, absorb the visual of that parade of beautiful girls. That made high school a lot more bearable.

73

Some of our teachers were real characters, and not always in a good way. They had all been educated during the Soviet times and they all adhered to the Soviet school of thought that children were not human, they didn't count.

It was like the military—you weren't allowed to open your dirty sewer unless you received explicit permission to do so. Or were ordered to speak.

One thing the teachers hadn't agreed on among themselves was whether chewing gum in class was okay or not. Some were adamantly against it and they made it clear the first day you met them. Other took a more relaxed approach and allowed it.

My English teacher had never even mentioned gum.

"What are you doing?" she asked me.

I was confused. "Nothing?"

"You're chewing gum!"

I got even more confused. She had never pointed out that she didn't allow it in her class.

The teacher walked over to me and opened her hand in front of my mouth.

"Spit it out!"

I did as I was asked, making sure the gum was accompanied by as much saliva as I could possibly produce on such a short notice. Little did I know that was a bad mistake.

The next thing I knew was, she took the gum—and my spit—and pushed it firmly in my hair. Right smack in the middle of the top of my head.

I was horrified.

"Why would you do that?" I asked.

"Now you'll never chew gum in my class again."

I'm sure no one would chew gum in her class every again.

I had to cut a huge chunk of hair out. To anyone who could see the top of my head, I looked like a freak for months until it evened out again.

Another interesting character was the computer sciences teacher. He was a bit of a pervert. Whenever someone needed help with the computer, he stood behind that student, reached over their shoulders with his hands and typed on the keyboard.

It didn't matter whether the student was male or female. He did it to everyone. And it made everyone very uncomfortable. But none of us had even heard of sexual harassment, so we didn't know how to react or to whom complain.

I really liked my physics teacher, even though I hated the subject he taught. He always had witty remarks.

"Ask questions, people, if you don't understand," he said. "I know people say that one idiot can ask more questions than a hundred wise men answer, but that saying is nonsense. Idiots don't ask questions; it's the smart people who do because they want to learn more."

I decided to live by that principle. I always wanted to know more about things that interested me, too.

74

Parties at people's apartments were the thing of the nineteen-nineties. We couldn't afford to go out much, so we sought out friends whose parents had left town for the weekend, and they had stayed behind.

Everyone brought cheap booze, anything they could afford or steal from their parents' liquor cabinets. The main drink was vodka because it was the cheapest, and it was the surest way to get drunk quickly. You could mix vodka with anything. Orange juice, sparkling water, tonic, whatnot. You could also drink it straight up. Anything to get wasted quickly.

One afternoon we were playing strip poker at my mother's place. She had gone somewhere, so I had all the freedom in the world. We were drinking, smoking the place up, and doing stupid things. Like playing strip poker.

Corey, Roscoe and Clark were all there. We also had George, who was Corey's friend, and Eliza and Maggie, a pair of girls who were best friends.

Eliza was beautiful, she had deep dark eyes, long brown hair, and a very sweet and captivating look.

Maggie was a blond girl with blue eyes. She had a burn scar on her cheek and neck from an accident she had had when she was a kid. She was nice, and she filled my heart with joy by her mere existence.

I wanted her.

Eliza was Corey's girlfriend, so the honor code dictated she was off limits. And when someone's off limits because of an ongoing relationship, then you don't even think about them sexually. But Maggie was single. Maggie was Roscoe's love interest, but they weren't an item at the time.

That made her fair game.

Interestingly we drank beer that afternoon. The vodka would come later on.

Suddenly, when George was all but naked already because he had hit a losing streak, he decided he needed to go home. He only had his socks on.

"You're forfeiting the game?" Corey shouted with a smile on his face. He had the most clothes on.

"I have to go home. My parents are waiting," George said, but it felt like a lie to all of us.

"Well, that calls for a punishment," I said. I just had no idea what it should be.

"It sure does," Corey seconded. "Let's see. Okay, you can leave if you take your socks off, too, and walk back and forth the apartment, completely naked, for five minutes."

We all cheered. That seemed like a reasonable punishment for quitting.

George had no choice. He obediently did what was asked of him, only to return ten seconds later to the living room where we all were sitting and continuing the game.

"The fucking dog had pissed on the floor!" he exclaimed. "I stepped into it with both of my feet!"

We were roaring with laughter. That had been the funniest thing happen that week, and we wouldn't let it go.

But a part of me felt sorry for George. That miserable dumb bastard of a dog had, again, peed in the apartment. And my new friend had stepped into that pee. That fucking animal.

I had to clean it up, too.

George washed his feet in the bathroom, got dressed and off he went.

We continued our game.

We didn't get any of the girls naked. Maggie had to take her bra off. The burn scar extended to her left boob.

It didn't matter to me. She had beautiful, exquisite boobs. I wanted to squeeze them. Put my face between them. Lick them. Kiss them.

I just didn't know how to approach her.

75

The girls we were trying to chase that day were gorgeous. But we were all drunk, and the girls weren't. Common sense dictated we were never going to catch them.

Besides, we needed to pee like hell.

"You can't properly fuck when you need to pee," Corey spread his wisdom. As if he knew. I was the only one of our group who had actually been with a woman. Let alone, I was the only one who had actually seen a woman naked. Other than one's mother or sister, that is. But I decided to let them have their illusions.

We never caught nor fucked the girls we had our eyes on. That was a shame, as these girls were gorgeous.

The guys were all virgins. But that didn't stop the word "virgin" from being an insult.

"You're a virgin," Clark told me every time we had a disagreement. It didn't matter if the disagreement was about a computer game or a brand of jeans. That was the go-to argument every time.

I didn't mind.

"You're only saying that because you're one," said. "I don't give a shit. You're the one who does."

He got offended. I liked that.

Fun times.

76

I had introduced my new friends, who lived around where I did, to my old ones—both Simon and Michael occasionally took part in our activities. We would meet up somewhere in the city, someone would by a bottle of vodka, and we'd just sit at some beautiful park, discuss the daily matters, lie about who we all had fucked that week, and drink.

Until that bottle was done. Then we'd walk to a liquor store, put all our money, the little that we had, together, and buy another one. It was entertainment for us. It was a liberating distraction from our every-day lives, something our parents didn't know or care about—well, they might have cared if they had known—and something our teachers in school had no control over.

It was the perfect setting of being young in a country that was just reinventing itself and wasn't enforcing any laws it had enacted.

It was illegal to buy cigarettes or booze if you were under eighteen. In theory. In practice, I could walk to a news stand and buy a pack of cigarettes. No one cared. I could walk to a liquor store and buy a bottle of vodka. No one fucking cared.

I loved my teenage years. My friends loved theirs, too.

One day, we were sitting on a hill near the old town, drinking beer and vodka together and feeling happy. I suddenly felt I needed to pee, so I wandered off to nearby bushes to relieve myself.

The cops showed up. It was still illegal to drink in the public. They rounded all of them up—sparing me because I was in the bushes—and tried to force everyone in the police cars.

But Michael was the one who wouldn't take it. He managed to get loose from a police officer's grip and just ran. He was the fastest runner any of us knew.

He just ran and off to the night he went.

The rest of the gang got arrested for drunken and disorderly behavior. Only Michael and I were spared.

Sometimes, your weak bladder is a blessing. Or, in Michael's case, your fast legs.

I went on wandering around the old town after my friends were arrested. I didn't know what else to do. I needed to sober up a bit before going home, but I was also worried about what would happen to my friends. Are they going to jail?

"Hey," I heard a whisper from a narrow alley.

"What?"

"Hey, it's me, Michael. Come here."

And there he was. Alive. He wasn't arrested. His fast legs had served him well. Thank fuck, I thought.

"Let's go bust those assholes out of jail!" Michael suggested, knowing full well that wasn't going to happen.

"The fuck do you mean? We can't bust them out of jail."

"Oh, well. Let's get another bottle of vodka then."

I was open to that suggestion. Fuck sobriety, I can deal with that another day, I figured.

Walking back from the nearest liquor store, there was a police car parked on the curb. I couldn't believe what happened next.

Michael went to the driver's side of the cop car, spit on the window, and screamed, "Boo! Pigs! Go fuck yourselves."

Those weren't even the same cops who had arrested our friends. But Michael was drunk, angry, and he wasn't afraid to show his resentment.

We were a rebellious crowd. We knew we were breaking the law; we just didn't give a shit.

The cop on the driver's seat jumped out of the car as quickly as he could, but it was too late. Michael's fast legs had already sent him sprinting to the territories unknown.

The cop even drew his sidearm when he was running after him, but about five minutes later, he returned to his car with bitter disappointment all over his face. That trained police officer wasn't fast enough for that sprinter high school kid.

Michael was in the clear.

I went home and fell asleep. I was so drunk. The adrenaline had helped, too.

77

We had another plan for an apartment party that night. At my apartment, again. More often than not, it seemed like my mother was the only one to ever fuck off so the apartment would be all mine.

I didn't mind that, though. The only thing I had to do was clean it up afterwards and keep the windows open long enough for the stink of tobacco smoke to leave.

We were in the old town again, getting pre-drunk for the party.

"Hey, Maggie, can I talk to you?" I asked her. She came to me.

I had finally worked up my courage to ask her.

"Would you be my girlfriend?"

She looked down.

"I kinda like another guy," she said.

Okay then. There wasn't much else I could do. I knew a woman always chooses her man, and if she doesn't choose you, there's nothing you can do.

But the other guy she liked wasn't Roscoe.

It was Michael.

Maybe I made a mistake introducing Michael to my neighborhood crew, I thought.

Sure, Michael was more handsome, better looking than I was. He was more masculine. And he sure could run.

He was definitely more handsome than Roscoe. The fact that Maggie chose Michael over Roscoe didn't surprise me at all. The fact that she chose Michael over me didn't either.

It just hurt.

They spent the entire afternoon together. At times, they even walked on the other side of the street from the rest of our gang.

I was hurt. I wasn't mad at Maggie or Michael, even though I wanted to be. Michael had become my best friend, I loved him, and I only wanted good things for him. A part of me wanted to hate him, wanted to disown him as a friend. But my brain kept reminding me that he had done nothing wrong.

I believed my brain. I didn't even tell him how it had hurt me. I just let it pass.

It was Maggie's choice and so be it.

We all went back to my place and got even more drunk.

As the night progressed, Corey and Eliza decided to do naughty things. They retired to my bedroom, while the party was going on in the living room.

Soon after, Michael and Maggie decided to do the same.

They were in the same queen-size bed, one couple on one side, the other couple on the other. Not exactly an orgy, but a strange setup for sure.

Neither of them could get it up, though. They had plans to fuck their respective girlfriends while in the same bed, nothing separating them, but those only remained that—plans.

"This is not going to get hard," I heard Maggie say through the wall.

Maybe it wasn't meant to be that night.

***

"What the fuck happened?" I later asked Michael.

"I was too drunk," he said.

Maybe. Or maybe it wasn't the best setting for an inaugural sex of a relationship.

Michael and Maggie ended up being together for some time. They made a beautiful couple. My disappointment subsided, too.

Corey and Eliza didn't end up being together for long. They were too different people.

78

The following morning was horrendous. I was hung over like hell, and the only thought in my head was, where were my smokes. With shaking hands, I felt all my pockets and found nothing there. Fuck, someone had smoked my cigarettes, I thought.

I always had the worst hangovers. Sometimes I puked my guts out and went back to sleep, sometimes I would feel the absolute need to vomit, but nothing came out.

That morning, I had a terrible headache. And I knew that the only way to escape the pain was just to continue drinking. Only the sick feeling in my stomach, the reflex that made even the smell of any booze repulsive, kept me from carrying on.

I wished I had at least beer somewhere. I wandered to the kitchen to check the refrigerator—nope, no beer. Fuck.

Then I looked around. Some of the party participants were asleep wherever they could find a spot. One was on the kitchen table. Well, he was sitting in a chair, leaning on the table and using his hands as a pillow.

The fuckbuddies from the previous night—or it may actually have been in the early hours of the morning—had gone to their respective homes. Someone else was sleeping in my bed. I didn't even know who it was.

I had slept on the living room couch where my mother slept when she was home. Someone was under the living room coffee table, on the carpet, seemingly dreaming peacefully.

The bathroom sink was full of someone's vomit. Lovely. I knew I was the one who had to clean it up.

The air was thick of cigarette smoke. I opened the windows to air the place up. I knew that would take a while.

Someone had burned a hole in one of the armchairs with a cigarette. It might have been me.

Then I loitered to the bathroom to pee. It wasn't one of those mornings I needed to violently puke.

Someone had broken the toilet bowl's water tank—it had come loose from the bowl itself and there was a huge crack in the bit that had held the tank to the bowl.

The entire bathroom smelled like pee. Someone had peed on the walls and the floor. But most importantly, that someone had peed on a copy of The Godfather that I kept there for my long dumps that would've otherwise been just very boring self-contemplation. I didn't want to contemplate anything when I was taking a dump, I read and reread and then reread again. It was The Godfather's time.

The doorbell rang. It was Corey.

"What the fuck happened here last night?" I asked him, showing him the destruction in the john.

"Oh, that was Clark," he said, sounding quite confident.

"How do you know?"

"I saw him, he had the door open. He pissed all over the place, then, I guess, he got tired and sat down on the shitter and leaned against the water tank. That's how he broke it."

I was furious at Clark. Who the fuck did he think he was, pissing all over my bathroom and breaking the water tank? And, most importantly, destroying my most favorite book in the entire world.

Another doorbell.

And there he was, the hero of the day. Clark, after what he had done the night before, had reappeared on my doorstep with a face on like nothing had happened?

"Seriously? You came back here after what you did last night?" I screamed.

He seemed baffled.

"What did I do?"

"You pissed all over my john! All over my Godfather book! And you fucking broke the shitter!"

Then I punched him in the face. With all my strength. I may have broken his nose. Served him right, I thought.

Clark and I stopped being friends there and then. When we saw each other in our neighborhood, we changed direction. I didn't want to be his friend because he had turned out to be an asshole. He didn't want to be my friend because he knew he was an asshole. Or so I thought.

79

Us being in the arts class, our class teacher was also our literature teacher. And one of the first assignments she gave us—her new class, so she'd get to know us—was to write a book.

I was a huge James Bond fan, so I decided to write a spy story. It was a horrendous one, very short, about a half-Chinese, half-English guy from Hong Kong who, walking in his father's footsteps, became a spy for the United Kingdom, and fought some enemies here and there.

Did I say it was a horrendous, shitty story? Because it was.

"The best of y'all's work was Elliot's," the teacher said after a few months when she had read all of our stories.

Really? My story was the best? How the fuck can that be?

"His was really thought through. It was almost enjoyable to read. Just one thing, Elliot. Don't curse all the time. Really, don't swear."

I was happy. I had actually done something really well.

I never stopped cursing, though. She was somewhat a prude, even though she was generally a really nice, really down-to-earth person. She just didn't like cursing.

"You need to keep on writing," she insisted. "You'll only get better. The only way you will become a writer is if you just keep on writing."

That I believed. And that I did.

But if my shitty story was the best among thirty-six, then how bad had the other ones been? I couldn't get that thought out of my head. The fuck are these people doing in an arts class to begin with?

80

We had parties at school, too. They were called discoes, but they were more like drooling by the boys and playing around by the girls, with only the few lucky boys getting to dance with the girls they wanted to dance with. Even less of the boys got to dance with the girls they wanted to fuck. And nobody ever fucked anybody, at the end of the day.

Mary was a year younger than my class. She mostly kept to herself, and she wasn't too interested in my attempts to hit on her.

In that party, though, I went full-on. Fuck it, I've got to score at least one dance with her.

She didn't want to. She was sitting in the corner, pretending to read a magazine in the dark.

I was persuasive. I really liked her. Maybe I did because she was an underdog like I was. Mary wasn't classically pretty. She had chicken pox scars all over her face. But she was pretty to me. I wasn't in love with her, but I liked her.

I didn't even think about fucking her. I just wanted to dance with her. And maybe, after we danced a bit and she got to know me, I would get to make sweet love to her, too.

Finally, dance we did. Just one song. It was a slow pop song, a waltz-like song, so we held hands and were physically close at times.

And then Mary decided that was it for her and she left, back to her corner, back to her magazine that she possibly couldn't read in the dark.

"You basically raped her," Charles told me. He had been watching me.

"Fuck you. I persuaded her. She's a nice girl, I like her."

"She didn't want anything to do with you, you just forced her to dance with you."

"So what?" I said. "I persuaded her to dance with me and she did."

"You're a rapist," Charles said.

He was just teasing me. "Wanna get a drink?"

We walked to a nearby grocery store. We didn't have much money.

We bought a bottle of whisky. The bottle claimed it was Scotch. Hence, whisky, without the "e."

It was called King Barley.

It was the most horrendous thing I had ever tasted.

Kevin, another temporary classmate, joined us, too.

We drank three pints of that horrendous swill between the three of us.

The next day, I was the only one of us who showed up at school. I was so hung over that I couldn't concentrate on anything. I just wanted to puke, shit, sleep, and then do all that over again.

Steve, who hadn't been there at the party the previous night, had a field day. He was very happy he hadn't been there. Otherwise, he would've been as hung over as I was.

Charles and Kevin stayed home, puking their guts out there.

Good for them, taking a sick day.

I actually fucking showed up even though I felt like I was dying, dead, resurrected, dying and dead again.

But it made me feel like a hero. At least to myself.

***

When we graduated from high school, our class teacher reminisced about our time with her.

"I never saw you drinking. But I did find bottles."

Charles and I were confident that had been the King Barley bottle. After all, we threw it in the class trash bin. It was the only item there when everyone returned in the morning.

When the class teacher said that, we smiled and looked at each other. The teacher knew at that moment that it had been us.

81

In the years after the Soviet occupation ended, the used car market opened up. People were selling, buying, trading in cars. People were traveling all over Europe to buy used cars, from huge car markets. My mother's dad took bus trips to Germany to buy cars, which he then drove back home, used them for a while, and then sold them—only to take another trip to Germany, to a massive car market, to buy another.

My father wouldn't have had the patience to do that. He just went out to a car market in Estonia and bought the first car he saw. He didn't know much about cars, he would just go and see if he liked something and then buy it. But, with his first Western car, he did really well.

The car he bought was the Peugeot 505, an old French car—exactly as old as me—and it was a great car. The French had, back in the day, the ability to produce good-looking cars, but most importantly, they were extremely comfortable cars. Even sitting in the back seat—let alone the front one—I felt like I'm sitting in a cotton ball. I could feel no pothole; the car just went through everything the roads had to offer so smoothly that the people in it couldn't feel a thing.

One day, my dad was traveling again somewhere and Corey had an idea.

"Let's take you dad's car and drive to my mother's house." His mother lived a few miles away, in a different neighborhood, with her new husband at the time.

"Fuck that," I said. "If I get caught with driving without a license, I will be fucked."

"You're not going to get caught," Corey promised. "It will be like any other day."

I contemplated it. If I were to get caught, I would be hit with a massive fine.

But if weren't, I'd be a hero in my new friends' world. Being a hero got the best of me.

I drove really slowly. Trying to keep up with the city traffic, but not standing out in any way.

"Hey, faster, faster," Corey said. He was jumping up and down in the front seat as if the ride had been the best day of his life.

"Calm the fuck down," I replied. "Let's keep our heads down, let's keep a low profile."

We made it to his mother's house. He went in. He got out. And we drove back.

This was the scariest car drive I had ever had. There I was, driving a car in a town of half a million people and who knows how many cars, without a license, with only the driving skills I had learned from my mother's father when I was twelve years old.

But nobody bothered us. We weren't pulled over. We didn't even see any cops, even though they were always around. We made it to Corey's mother's place, and we made it back. Without incident.

Needless to say, I was really fucking proud of myself. And I knew that if my father—or my mother, for that matter—ever found out, I'd be fucked six ways from Sunday.

Nobody talked. It was like omertá, the Sicilian code of silence. No one of our crew ever mentioned it again.

That suited me well.

82

Michael and I arrived late at that apartment party. It was held in the apartment of one of Roscoe's classmates from high school. Roscoe himself was there, of course, and Corey, and George. A few friends of Lester, the classmate of Roscoe, too. And Roger, Corey's semi-friend who wanted so hard to be a bully, but he never realized he didn't possess enough intelligence.

Even though he was rather dumb, Roger was a proper asshole. He was fat, tall, and yet, he thought a world of himself. He wanted to bully everyone—even Corey—but Corey wouldn't take any bullshit from anyone, and so they had ended up being semi-friends rather than enemies. They seemed to tolerate each other, but that was the extent of their relationship.

Roger tried to bully me, too. Even wannabe bullies have an eye for potential victims.

I just told him to go fuck himself. That did the trick. As I said, he wasn't too smart.

One time, while drinking heavily, of course, Corey had told Roger he was a piece of shit. Corey was ready to fight him, if need be, but the need never arose.

Roger started crying instead.

"A piece of shit?" he asked through his tears. "Nobody has ever said anything this mean to me. My own friend? Calling me a piece of shit?" It was almost heartbreaking to watch him cry and sulk in his own piece-of-shitness.

But he really was a piece of shit. Hence "almost."

The one thing Roger had was money. I don't know where he got it, but I doubted its source was a legal one. And he had decided to use his money to call hookers to the party. When Michael and I arrived, some of them had already had their pleasure while some others were still working on it.

Corey was walking around with a fedora he had found in Lester's clothes' cabinet.

"Yeah. I fucked her. She even used her mouth to put on the condom."

He was on top of his world. He had finally lost his virginity. With a vodka bottle in his hand, he kept walking around the apartment, winking at everyone, making small talk, and just being so happy with himself as if he had just won a million units of hard currency.

I guess it's a big thing, losing your virginity, even if it is to a hooker.

"Hey, Elliot," Roger called out for me. "If I paid for it, would you fuck a hooker?"

"Keep your money, Roger," I said. "I would never fuck a hooker. I would never fuck for money."

***

That was a lie, though.

I had once paid for fucking. Just the one time, but I did.

After yet another drunken escapade at someone's apartment, I was walking home through the old town. And suddenly, a girl approaches me.

"You want to have fun?"

I shrugged. "What do you have in mind?"

"For twenty-five crowns, anything."

Wow, I thought.

She wasn't particularly pretty. An average-looking girl with brown hair and green eyes, just hooking the streets of the town, making money that way. I figured, why not.

We walked to a nearby park. It was in the middle of the night, it was completely dark, no one would catch us.

I had her the twenty-five crowns she asked for. I wasn't sure what I would get. An official call girl—one with a pimp and possibly a place of work—would be three hundred crowns per hour.

She took my dick out of my pants and blew me nicely. Not professionally, not even passionately, but nicely. I didn't need to complain.

"Fuck me in the ass," she then said. "I really like being fucked in the ass."

I did. I didn't mind. After all, she specifically requested it, so who was I to decline.

When I pulled out after I came, she turned around.

"It looks like I made your dick dirty," she said. "May I clean it up?"

I nodded.

She polished it really well. I even contemplated not taking a shower.

I still did. Just in case. I didn't know what kind of bacteria lurked around her mouth if she did that daily.

Mouths are the breeding grounds of bacteria. I would never share a toothbrush.

She was a nice girl, probably just fallen on hard times. She was twenty-five crowns richer; I was one load poorer. Everybody won.

83

At times, my brother Danny got really fed up with my teasing and torturing. He was too small to do anything about it but tell our parents about this or that that I had done to him. Then the parents would yell at me or punish me, which only worked until the next time.

That day, Corey, Roscoe and I were sitting in front of our apartment building, smoking cigarettes and planning our next drunken escapades. Danny was playing in the yard with the dumbass dog.

For some reason, we figured it would be funny to throw small stones at the Danny. Really small, they wouldn't harm him if they had hit him.

"Hey, stop that!" he shouted.

We were having fun and didn't want to.

"I'm serious! I'm going to tell mom!" That made it even more hilarious.

It's all fun and games until someone gets hurt. That day, that someone ended up being me.

The same blind rage that sometimes overcame me, it overcame Danny. He grabbed the biggest rock he could find from the ground and threw it at us.

The rock hit me right in my forehead. Fuck me, that kid could become a hell of a baseball player, I could have thought, except I didn't because I didn't know what baseball was.

The blood was flowing. Head wounds are always bad; this one had penetrated all layers of my skin and the blood just kept on dripping.

I felt a bit woozy, but I managed to run upstairs to my third-floor apartment, with the help of my friends. I was holding the wound with my hand, but the blood kept on coming, leaving a trail of thick red blood drops on every step.

Even Gary's evil stepmother ran out of her apartment, to see what the commotion was about.

"Oh my god, you're bleeding all over the hallway!" she screamed. But she did feel sorry for me, too. "Wait, let me get some ointment."

Fuck, great. What kind of sorcery would she come up with, I thought.

She ran into her apartment and returned with a small bottle of what looked like ink. For all I knew, it could have, indeed, been ink. The fuck was she going to do, give me a tattoo?

She poured it on a cotton ball and tried to squeeze it against my wound.

"Let me put this on you, it will stop the bleeding!"

"Get the fuck away from me, you crazy bitch," I screamed at her. I didn't want to end up with a blue ink spot on my forehead.

But I was dizzy and couldn't fight her off so easily. She pushed the blue cotton ball against my wound.

"Hold it here for a while," she said.

I was too weak to say no, so I did. But the ink didn't do shit. The blood kept pouring out of my head.

I threw the cotton ball away and got a new, clean one from our bathroom. After some half an hour, I finally stopped the bleeding.

The wound looked hideous. It wasn't even symmetric. Why would it be, if an unsymmetric rock created it, I thought.

I bandaged myself up.

"Guys," I said to my friends, "thanks for your help. I'm going to go lie down for a while. I doubt I'll be doing a lot of drinking tonight."

"That's okay," Corey said. "Get some rest."

"Thanks."

They left and I went and laid down.

It taught me a valuable lesson. Never fuck with someone who had superpowers you don't know about. Danny had the superpower of almost killing me. I thought twice after that incident whether to torture him or just leave him be.

84

Michael and I had grown to be best friends. We did everything together. We went to parties together, we tried to pick up girls—mostly unsuccessfully—together, we drank together, and we smoked together.

I had been the one who taught him to smoke. Maybe that wasn't my finest hour. But I didn't know better.

One night we were just aimlessly wandering around the town, walking as we always did, until we ended up by the beach. The night had fallen upon us already and we really had nowhere to go other than home.

But we hadn't had a single drink yet that night. That needed to be corrected.

"How much money do you got?" I asked Michael.

"Not sure. Let me check."

He had some crowns and some cent coins.

I didn't have much more either.

We counted the money carefully and realized we had exactly the amount of money that would buy us a pint of the cheapest vodka, and a pint of sparkling water to flush the vodka down.

So there we were, in the middle of the night, four miles away from my home and ten from Michael's, sitting at a bus stop and drinking vodka and sparkling water straight from the bottle. We had to drink the water sparingly because we only had the pint—and flushing down a pint of vodka with only a pint of water can be challenging.

The last half a pint of the vodka, we drank that straight up.

There wasn't a single person around. Not one car drove by the bus stop. It was the dead of night. Everyone seemed to be asleep, other than the two kids at that bus stop.

"Okay, it's time to go home now," I suggested.

So we walked the four miles back to my place.

"You can stay here," I told Michael. "Go home in the morning."

He tried. He turned from one side to the other on the couch for half an hour and then got up.

"Fuck it. I'm going home."

"It's the middle of the fucking night," I said. "Sleep here."

He didn't listen.

Later I learned he had walked another mile to the train station, slept there on a wooden bench and taken the first train of the day home.

My couch would've been more comfortable than the wooden bench at the train station. But who was I to judge.

85

Corey's grandmother had a summer cottage not far from the town. When we got sick of the apartment parties—especially in the summer—we'd all go to Corey's grandma's summer cottage instead. It was a small cottage, but had a big garden, so we could spread around nicely in the yard and enjoy our drinks in a much bigger space.

My birthday was coming up, but my mother wasn't planning on going anywhere, so I lacked the options as to where to hold my birthday party.

"Hold it at my summer cottage," Corey suggested.

"Really? You wouldn't mind?"

"Let it be my gift to you," he said.

"Wow. Thanks."

So it was settled.

I invited my friends to the party and everyone brought some booze. My grandmother had prepared some foods for us to enjoy. Corey invited some of his friends whom I didn't know, too. I didn't mind. It was his—well, his grandma's—cottage, so he had the right.

He also invited his cousin Rose.

I was smitten with her. She was a tall girl—taller than me—and she had dark blond hair and blue eyes. She looked like a supermodel, but she wasn't one. She had a brain, and girls who had brains didn't become the representatives of an occupation that demanded none.

I had always been turned on by smart girls. Stupid girls—good for occasional fucking, but nothing else. Smart girls were relationship material.

We talked most of the night, but as the night progressed, I got more and more drunk. To a point where I didn't remember anything. After all, it was my birthday, so it was my right to drink myself to the oblivion.

***

"This was the best party I ever attended," Corey said to me the next morning with a big smile on his face. We were cleaning up the cottage. The guests had left.

Some booze was still left over, so that made the hangover less and the cleaning up more fun.

"What do you mean?"

"You don't remember anything, do you?"

I had no idea what I was supposed to remember. The fuck did I do, I asked myself.

And then I asked Corey.

"The fuck did I do?"

"Oh. The question is, the fuck you didn't do."

I begged him to tell me.

"You got your dick out in front of Rose and asked her to blow you. As if you'd ever get it hard, in the state you were."

What the fuck. How could I have been so disrespectful to a woman, especially a woman I liked? That didn't sound like me, I thought.

"That was not all. You ran after her all around the garden with your dick swinging. Yelling, 'blow me, blow me.'"

I had absolutely no recollection of that.

"This is bullshit," I said. "You're just outright bullshitting me. I would never do that."

"Ask anyone. You did. You were so blotto you couldn't believe."

Corey couldn't stop laughing at me and my swinging dick. He didn't even mind I had treated his cousin this way. The entire situation had amused the shit out of him.

He could be right, I thought. I didn't remember almost anything from the previous night.

Later I would ask a few people who had attended the party. They all confirmed Corey's story.

I was embarrassed.

I never saw Rose again. That was a crying shame. But I deserved it.

86

My mother had started a new business—she was teaching English. She had gathered a solid client base and at one point it had gotten too big for her to manage, so she thought, why not give some of those clients to me.

I was happy. I spoke good English, I was strong in both the grammar and the vocabulary, and my mom had all the textbooks necessary, so why not. And I would make my own money again, money I could use to buy booze and cigarettes.

I was happy.

Until I found out who the people were I was supposed to teach.

Many were nice, decent people. Some were complete imbeciles.

There were a couple of intelligence officers of the defense forces. They carried their guns in their fanny packs.

I couldn't get that image out of my head. You're a supposed James fucking Bond, and you walk around with a fanny pack where you carry your gun, among the rest of your shit.

At least they were trying to learn English. How they had become intelligence officers without knowing a word of English was another mindblowing thing about them. But there they were, their guns in their fanny packs and not speaking a word of English.

I did my best. They probably didn't have their best. They weren't lazy like I was in school. They tried as hard as they could. And they would eventually fall out of the group and go their own way.

If the Estonian intelligence services are built up on people like that, we have no future, I thought. I was wrong, though. Maybe in due course morons like that were fired from the intelligence services and they had to seek employment in fields more suitable for them. Trench digging, street sweeping, maybe emptying septic tanks.

But I did end up with having a group of two lovely girls as students. They were in their twenties when I was in my teens. After all, I was still in high school. There was something satisfying about teaching a new skill to people older than me—and all my students were older than me.

And there was something even more satisfying teaching girls older than me. It could show them I was as smart as handsome. If I only were handsome.

I was in love with both of them. But I never hit on either of them. It would have been a breach of professional ethics. After all, I was supposed to teach them, not try to fuck them.

At nights, though, the mental images of them provided me with plenty of material to jerk myself off to sleep.

Good times.

87

Michael and Maggie had broken up months earlier.

Maggie had found that she liked Roscoe more than she liked Michael.

Nobody really liked Roscoe. He was a pathological liar who invented stories to make himself feel better. We just hung around with him. Maybe Maggie saw something else in him. Fuck if we knew.

He told everyone the shitty green Mazda his mother was driving was manufactured at a Porsche factory. We all knew this was bullshit. But we let him lie because it made him feel good and we didn't give a shit. Let him live in his own world, filled with bullshit stories that he actually may have believed.

Corey was dating Trina. A nice, kind girl, quite short. Not to my taste at all, but that wasn't in the equation anyway. I made it my business not to hit on girls who were in a relationship. Especially in a relationship with a friend of mine.

"You know what happened last night?" Corey told us. "I was in my room, my hand in Trina's machine, when my grandma walks in. She looks around and says, 'Why isn't Trina wearing any pants?' I mean, what the fuck did she think we were doing there?"

We chuckled. Old people were funny, we thought. My grandmother had once told me that sex, like cigarettes, stopped your growth. I had replied, "Oh, well, then I should be a midget." She didn't bring up bullshit like that ever again.

It was a common belief—or a scaring tactic—in the Soviet Union to tell kids that if they smoke, their growth would stall and they'll be midgets.

Corey and Trina seemed happy together. Until things started to fall apart.

Trina had taken a liking to Michael. And Michael didn't mind.

For a while, she went back and forth from Corey to Michael and from Michael to Corey. But she liked Michael better, so she stayed with him. Corey was heartbroken, even though he didn't show that. He was angrier at Michael than he was at Trina.

None of us could understand that it was the woman's choice with whom she wants to be. We all thought we were these alpha males, possessing the women we dated or just fucked, without realizing they weren't ours because we wanted them to be, but because they wanted them to be ours. And they could change their minds any time.

Trina had changed her mind and that made Corey furious. And the making-up process between Corey and Michael wasn't pleasant, either.

"Head or gut?" Corey asked Michael. He had gotten that from a Bruce Willis movie, called "The Last Boy Scout."

"Gut," Michael said, making the only reasonable choice. Corey punched him in the gut as strongly as he could.

He would later go around, claiming Michael crouched and coughed and almost puked his guts out to his punch.

Michael did crouch a bit. But it wasn't even half as dramatic as Corey made it out to be.

And there they were. The pecking order of the wannabe alpha males was restored. Corey got his revenge and got to tell his version of the revenge to everyone; Michael got the girl and was surely happier than Corey, despite the brief pain that ensued the punch.

Everyone was happy again.

88

"I have to tell you something," our class teacher said on September 1, 1995, the first day of school that fall—and the first day of the twelfth grade, our final year in high school. "The month of May is right around the corner."

May was when we were all supposed to graduate. She wanted to motivate us to screw our heads on right and do whatever it took to study quickly, to get ready for the finals and realize that the last year of high school would pass extremely quickly, faster than we would realize.

She was right. Sure as shit, the month of May was right there. The spring was in the air, the trees and the bushes were blossoming, and we were getting ready to be grownups, actual human fucking beings responsible for our lives and futures.

"Drink responsibly," she told us when we had received our diplomas and embarked to the short bus ride to where we had chosen our graduation party to be held.

We did no such thing, of course.

All of my classmates were eighteen, and they were legally allowed to drink. I, the youngest in the class, was only seventeen.

Nobody cared, though. I was poured every drink I asked for.

I had set my eyes on another girl in our class. She was short, shorter than the most of us. She had a dark skin, like a gypsy. She had short hair like a boy. She had always been like that, throughout high school. A kindhearted, pretty tomboy. Some guys at school thought she was a lesbian.

The guys felt differently about lesbianism than we did about faggotry. We knew faggotry had been a heavily punishable in the Soviet Union and that had formed our opinions very negatively. It had to be something god-awful if it was banned and people went to prison for it.

But the idea of lesbianism was taken one of two ways by us. Some thought it was equally disgusting as faggotry, and others thrived on lesbian pornography. There may have been middle ground, too—guys who publicly denounced it and at night jerked off to girl-on-girl porn in their favorite dirty magazine.

Once we had flicked through a few porn magazines with my cousin John.

"I really don't like those," he said when he saw a photo of two women pleasuring each other orally.

I shrugged. I didn't feel one way or another. They didn't turn me on, but I didn't think they were gross either.

But I didn't believe the girl at the party was a lesbian. I had always liked her.

We danced a few dances while I kept drinking. She didn't drink much.

"You wanna go somewhere else?" I asked her in the middle of a dance.

"Like where?"

"I don't know."

There was a winter garden right next to our party venue, full of palm trees and other tropical plants no one knew the names of. No one cared, either.

I suggested we go there. She agreed.

We spent a beautiful night together. Until she realized she had well overstayed her curfew and had to go home. She ran off without saying goodbye, hailed a cab and off she was.

I never saw her again.

***

I kept on drinking. All the guys in our class—the six of them—kept drinking and hitting on the girls who didn't drink nearly as much as we did. Some of them got lucky, some didn't.

Charles had left the party with one of the girls I had immensely liked. They ended up walking on the beach, deep at night, where they realized they liked each other and fucked each other's brains out.

I had already gotten my brains fucked out.

Nothing else mattered.

I sat in the bar, looking at the drunken animals with whom I had gone to school for the past three years—and some for the past twelve years—and imbibed, drink after drink.

School had been hell. High school, a different kind of hell, but outside of it, I had experienced much more than I could have imagined.

Inside of it was a different story. I'd rather not remember that story. Good thing the brain has the capability of blocking bad memories, I thought.

I kept drinking until I fell into the oblivion. I didn't remember much what happened after that. A lot of it had darkness. Maybe I had died. For all I knew, it may have been so.

***

In the morning, it was morning, and I was still alive.

Maybe I'll write a novel, I thought.

And then I did.

ACKNOWLEDGEMENTS

First and foremost, I want to thank my wife, Ingrid. She's always believed in me, she's been my muse, and she's also been my fiercest critic. Without her, I wouldn't have written and rewritten and then rewritten again anything I ever wrote, including this book. She has always tried to make me a better writer, and I'd like to think she's succeeded—thanks to her, I am better than the normal, lazy me would be.

I love my son, Brett, very much and I'm most grateful to him for having been born and giving me the chance to be a role model to someone—even if not such a good one, at least at times. But I'm grateful for who you are, and I hope this book will show you that you can take all experiences you get in your life, no matter how bad or good they've been, and all that you learn, and turn them into something better, something new, something beautiful, something satisfying. The only thing that matters is what you think. You can accomplish anything you put your mind into.

I'd like to thank my editor, Silver Tambur, my friend and my colleague in another endeavor we've undertaken together, the online magazine Estonian World (estonianworld.com). I think our relentless badgering of each other about anything and everything we write has made us both better writers, better editors, and it has also enhanced our sense of criticism—and tolerance.

Before meeting me, Silver used to think everyone was beautiful and good. I think I managed to show him that the world is quite the contrary—everyone's ugly and bad. Before meeting Silver, I used to think the world is full of assholes, that ninety percent of people are idiots. He has proved to me that only eighty-nine percent of people are idiots and, that even though the entire world is full of assholes, if you're more open minded, you can find hidden gems of people among the ocean of assholes that are actually good human fucking beings. I struggle.

My high school literature teacher, the late Ene Liivaste, who always told me to keep writing, to never quit—I'm sorry I was such an asshole to you on occasions. I didn't appreciate you at the time, but I sure as shit do now. You taught me valuable life lessons, and you also inspired me to keep on writing, to put my passion, my talent—the little I have—into my writing. I'm eternally grateful to you. I'm just sorry I didn't get the chance to tell you that in person. Maybe we'll meet again in heaven—or in hell. I really don't know which path we're going to go down. Hope you're up there; won't blame you if you're down there.

My mother provided quite a lot of subject matter for this book, and I'm grateful for that, too. You weren't a bad mother. You just didn't know how to be one. We are who and what we are. Genetics matter, too. Then again, she said I wrote well, after reading this book before its publication. Maybe she understands.

Much of that goes for my father, too. He, too, didn't really know how to be one. He wasn't a bad father, either. In fact, there were times I related with my father more than with my mother. But the most important part is, my father's father is who influenced the present me the most. I grew up to be my father's father. And maybe my father also has a role in that.

I would also like to thank everybody who might recognize themselves in this book. Many of you were and continue to be good, and I love you. Some of you, I needed to learn to know better, maybe we needed to grow up some more, and I needed to realize that if you really were assholes, you were just my kind of assholes.

And some of you were—and continue to be—assholes, and not my kind. I just hope you won't kill me after reading this book (if you can read, of course. I'm fairly sure many of you can't.) Also, I do have a few firearms. Just so you know.

Life is beautiful.

Made in the USA
Las Vegas, NV
21 December 2022

63711843R00109